CW00926227

The Babylon Chronicles

Chronicles

By

Henry Sipes

Enjoy!
Henry R. Sipes

Copyright

ISBN: 9798869007612

Independently Published

Illustration credits: The cover and graphics have been created by @Dedi5un, with minor contributions by Ryan Boatman and the author.

Table of Contents

Chronicle I: Babylonian Lines

The Beginning

Salaam Rahal remembered the vast plains of sand. The swirling eddies would slowly change the landscape, shifting its form into some unrecognizable creature that snaked its way across the desert. The sandstorms could make the beast a raging dragon as it roared flames across the dunes.

There was beauty there. Some would only see desolation. Some could watch the transformations in awe. Salaam saw beauty, from the tiny grains of sand playfully bouncing over each other to the mountainous storms sucking the sand off the floor into a rage of disdain for the creatures below.

As he viewed the asteroid's rocky gray craters and mountains before him, he found the same peace as in his home in Iraq. It was all the creation of Allah. If one could look with an open heart, everything Allah created was filled with glorious wonders and depths of beauty.

Salaam was at peace with the land and himself. He was a rugged individual with craters here and there on his face, resulting from a terrible acne infection as a teenager. There had been a time when he had grown a beard to cover his face. Some of the ladies would comment on how distinguished he looked. None would ever take his calls later.

Credit: Ryan Boatman

Taller than some but shorter than others, nothing made him stand out. Except, Salaam was darker than most Arabs back home. He was referred to by some as the darkness of shabib. He was, however, filled with a light that could not be extinguished. He had the knowledge and wherewithal to fuse thorium to replace the black gold that had plagued the Earth for centuries. Crude oil and coal.

His peers respected him for his knowledge. However, they had all been happy to see him leave. For the mission, he had been the obvious choice. A genius but an outcast that no one would miss. What better candidate for a mission to Psyche than someone whose name meant peace?

Salaam looked up at the stars and remembered when the outpost had first begun to search for data. The United Arab Emirates (UAE) was taking a huge financial risk to begin construction without a destination. He had upchucked more than once or twice in his suit, looking up at the stars back then as the asteroid rotated every four hours. They were not used to the dizzying stars flying above them. That had been one of the first things accomplished when they had established their thorium drives on the asteroid, eliminating its wobble and slowing it down to match the 24-hour rotation of the Earth.

𒐜

Pulling through the cavities of the vessel, running wires and tubes kept her mind off things back home. The energy crisis had reached the pinnacle of no return. There was only one way to go; a cataclysmic collapse. The darkness that fueled the Earth turned the spicket off with not so much as a drop to fall. Sara had jumped at the chance for a seat on the mission.

"Lafeete, how long will you be squirreling around in those tunnels?"
Sara jerked at Calager's voice and slammed her head into a truss.

"For the love of God, McGeen, you scared the hell out of me! Like, give a lady a warning first. Yaa knows, like a few soft beeps. You know how quiet it is over here. Until we fire the reactor, it's a coffin."

"My apologies, oh princess of the dead! Just a heads up, Salaam took one of his leisurely strolls this morning. In case he gets lost again, be prepared for a bit of a stroll yourself."

"10-4"

The stars slowly fading from Sara's vision reminded her of another collision between her head and something hard. One of her hobbies in France had been spelunking through the Dévoluy mountain range. As a petite woman, she had found it easy to crawl through some of the tightest spaces. The only thing that had kept her from exploring more than half of the 600 caverns in the range was her hard head. Or, as some would tease her, that it wasn't hard enough.

Sara had gotten into a tight spot deep in the Chourum des Aiguilles. Her helmet had got her stuck between a rock and, well, a hard place. Removing the helmet had seemed like the thing to do at the time until a cave critter made her jump. That had put her caving days on hold to heal the gash in her forehead. *I would have been just fine if not for that darn cave scorpion. But hey, all that caving experience, and not to mention my degree in electromechanical technology, got me this gig.*

"*Beep, beep, beep.* Sara, are you there?"

"Very funny, Calager. Yes, I am still here."

"I've lost Salaam's GPS signal. If I do not get a ping in the next hour, it might be time for a little lite exercise."

"Lite? The last time we had a workout together, I missed three work frames. I could not even sit up in bed!"

"We are just walking in suits, Sara. This is not a training exercise."

"Why the training anyway? We've been on this rock a long time; nobody is coming to pound us into the regolith. I'm not even one of your squad; I'm a tech."

"Hey, you asked for some workouts. I need everyone to be in top shape. They will come one day. Now get your ass over here!"

"Calager, it is going to take a bit. I'm about half a mile from the exit of this cable run."

Salaam, Salaam, Salaam, ever the dreamer. Dreaming is going to get you killed one day.

Salaam approached the rise of the next crater in great anticipation of what he would see beyond. He never tired of the landscape. He felt like one of the first explorers of the Antarctic. Sure, to the layman's eye, it was just a bunch of blinding white snow. To the first, it was a new land with wonders above and beneath. On Psyche, every crater was a new land to explore. Every time Salaam entered one, he knew he was the first *human* to set foot there.

He approached the crater rim with a bit too much enthusiasm and tripped over a boulder at the top. The gravity was so low on Psyche that he did not immediately fall but launched himself into a slow arc to land face down in the regolith of the crater. It was a soft landing, but not for his GPS unit. Salaam did not realize it, but the regolith short-circuited his unit as the tiny dust particles broke through. Psyche was metal-rich. The designers of the suit components had been aware, but only some of the quality checks had caught the seal issues related to foreign metals.

Turning to face the stars, he chuckled, thinking of his days playing in the sands back home. He would spend hours launching himself from dunes and tumbling down to the next. The ever-shifting sands had provided a soft landing. *There was that one time when I hit that rock.* His mom had scolded him for an hour while carefully cleaning the sand from the gash on his forehead. Absent-mindedly, Salaam raised his arm to rub his forehead only to realize he was massaging the outside of his helmet's face shield.

Credit: Henry Sipes

He slowly picked himself up and began to explore his surroundings. Looking across the flat terrain of the crater floor, he saw a few rocks that seemed to be placed in a pattern pointing toward a star. *I know, I know, it is probably random, but I must check.* He sauntered over to the rocks, hoping their locations would be too precise for anything other than intelligent life. He was always searching. There had to be some sign.

One last step, and he could begin to measure their alignment. He felt a vibration in his suit as he reached the first rock. He shrugged it off as it was probably his circulation fan again. *That darn thing. I've got to get Sara to check it out again.* Salaam mounted the laser to the first boulder and moved to the second to set up a receiver. It was not a perfect method, as the placement on the boulder's center was an educated guess, but it would give him some idea of how perfectly the stones were aligned. Before he reached the second, he felt the vibration again, only more substantial this time. *That was no fan. Oh, crap!*

It was too late. Salaam realized what was happening but could not turn to run away fast enough. The crater floor opened right in line with the boulders and directly beneath his feet. He threw out his pickaxe to grab anything where it could bite and stick, but it just slipped through the regolith at the edge of the fissure. The massive rift widened too fast to try again as he fell into the darkness of Psyche. Floating down, he realized the one thing he had not considered. Previous quakes had probably rolled those boulders down to the surface near the rift. *Intelligent life, how about I use some of my own intelligence? Salaam, you dream too much. There is no sign. It is a useless endeavor to continue to search.*

ᚻ|||

Calager McGeen was a hard man chiseled directly out of granite, Salaam would tell him. He maintained his rock-solid physique by working out in the 1 g accelerator. If not for his impulsiveness, he would never have had this opportunity to visit another world. Being kicked out of the Navy nuclear submarine program for proposing a new reactor using thorium, he had made himself an outcast. Well, bumping into the Admiral's daughter may have helped expedite his demise.

Calager looked up from the communication console as Sara exited the airlock. He gave her one look, and she knew what it meant.

"You know he is sitting there resting against some boulder, just gazing at the stars," she said.

"Let's hope so. Either way, his leisurely strolls are over."

"Calager, you are the one that set up these strolls to give people some time to themselves. A bit of *priv-a-see*, I think you pronounced it."

"I know, I know, I'm going to regret it, I'm afraid."

Credit: Ryan Boatman

Calager already had his suit on as Sara refilled her air tanks. He pulled his helmet over his head, and they each checked the other's suit as was protocol before exiting into the vacuum of Psyche. Sara checked her gauges one more time and commented, "I will be so excited to have the control tunnels under a pressurized atmosphere. A mile of crawling through the wiring tunnels makes a lady stink in these suits."

"Sara, it will not be long. Besides, only you can smell yourself in the suit. And for the moment, it helps that you are already suited to save us some time. Let's get going; it is only three klicks to where he left the rover."

"Three klicks? Do you mean we have to walk almost two miles in a suit? I am going to kill him!" Sara gave him the disgruntled look he had seen all too many times as they entered the airlock.

꘎ꛧꛧꛧꛧ

Salaam checked his oxygen readouts and sighed. *At least I will not suffocate.* It then occurred to him that suffocation may have been the way to go. It would have been a calm drop off into the la-la-land of sleep. It was a better alternative to what was coming. Now, he would slowly roast to death. What NASA had not seen with their first probes was hiding beneath the surface, something at the core of Psyche. The metal layers deep from the surface shielded the core. The UAE's probe, just by luck, had landed near one of these fissures and got a glimpse of the center.

Psyche had a molten core. No UAE astrogeologist could explain it. The core was molten thorium.

As he continued to slowly float down the fissure to the core, Salaam realized there was another way to die. He checked the time on his heads-up display, calculating how much time was left. There was another odd thing about Psyche related to these fissures. They opened and closed like clockwork. *Well, fantastic; I will not roast after all. I will just be smashed slowly like a tin can. Forgot about that way to die here.* One would have thought that with the slow speed of his float toward the core, Salaam could have tried the pickaxe several times to catch the sides and prevent his inevitable demise. The nature of the fissures did not allow this as they opened to a precise 30 feet across. Even if he could have reached the sides, they were a hard, unknown metal. They were also as smooth as glass to boot.

𒀭

"Calager to Salaam, over! Calager to Salaam, over!" Calager kept trying to raise Salaam with no luck. "Sara, you are the technical genius here. Any thoughts?"

"If his GPS unit is on the fritz… unless we have some line of sight, the extreme reflective metals make it impossible to get a laser signal. And you and I both know radio hasn't a chance.

Salaam is probably just enjoying the view, sipping some energy cocktail. Unless…"

"Do not even suggest it, Sara. No way Salaam would be dumb enough to go near them."

"Ah, sir, you know he is always looking for some evidence, some sign of life."

"Sara, can you make this thing go faster?"

"Calager, you know if we move faster and hit a bump, we could launch ourselves into orbit. That would be the best scenario. If we go too fast, we might just leave the system. You are sure this is the direction he went?"

"This was the excursion plan he logged this morning." Calager had triple-checked before they had left to be sure.

Looking up at the stars as he floated down to the fiery depths below, Salaam could see The Follower, ad-dabaran. He distinctly remembered an old poem his mother used to read.

I arrived haphazardly when ath-Thuraya, high overhead, was like an aquatic bird soaring.

Its rear parts – the Follower – flying in her tracks, yet neither falling behind
nor overtaking her,

With twenty small stars as if they – and he in the sky if he could speak –

Were camels that he led riding widespread, riding camels that were

about to scatter away from him,

Both connected and dispersed, and One Urging drives them to the water

From the heart of the spacious desert on their first night of travel.

It suddenly occurred to Salaam why he remembered this poem from the Umayyad poet, Dhu r-Rumma. Water. As the body's temperature rises, it tells the brain it needs water. Salaam's wandering thoughts had forgotten his dire situation – temperature. He looked at the display he had been trying to ignore: 95F. Rechecking the time, he sighed. *It's not going to be quick, Salaam. No tin can bone-crushing finale. You are going to roast like a Quzi. Oh, perhaps not, as it took Mother an entire day to prepare that lamb feast.* Salaam noted that the temperature was rising exponentially.

Having excellent knowledge of all things related to energy was not necessarily comforting in a situation like this. When he had been a young boy at school in Iraq, they had been taught about the dangers of their bodies overheating. He knew, at this point, that his body was handling his heat by sweating. Up to a point, his suit's cooling system would handle this. Up to a point… Once he approached approximately 100 degrees, his body would begin to struggle.

Salaam did some quick math based on the temperature rise and figured he had about five minutes before reaching that point. He quickly told his suit to excrete some meds in his water. His next concern was nausea. *I hit that wall, and it's going to get a bit smelly in here.* If the meds were insufficient, he would begin vomiting, and diarrhea would follow. He prayed to Allah that his brain would trigger fainting before he reached the next wall: cooked organs.

𒀭𒐊

Credit: Henry Sipes

Sara had reached down and pulled a wire from the speed governor's control while Calager had been busy trying to raise Salaam. It was a risk, but she was doing her best to avoid any piles of regolith or boulders that would serve as ramps into space. Driving the rover in her suit was making this task difficult. They had removed their helmets but stayed suited to act quickly in case Salaam was in trouble. There was another reason; Sara was pushing the speed limit. She knew all too well the capabilities of Salaam's suit, but she tried to ignore the thought. *If that crazy man has gotten himself into a fissure…*

Calager reached over and put his hand on Sara's. "We will be no help to him if we never make it. That was only a rhetorical question about going faster earlier. I've read the suit specs, as well. Knowing your equipment's capabilities is part of all space op training. The best we can do for him is get there and act immediately."

So much for passing out. Allah, where are you now? So, it is going to be cooked organs, then! The temperature inside was already reaching 105F. UAE had designed the suits to handle the typical temperature range between 225F and -250F. Even at the closest point to the sun with total exposure on the surface, -170F would be a lucky high. But closer to the core of Psyche, the temperature would rise much higher than 250F. *Great, now my*

lower back pain has returned. Salaam's brain was already beginning to fail. He should have remembered that the kidneys would go first. Before his brain could even consider the pain in his back, his body temperature was 110F. His suit's alarms wailed, but his brain could not register them. Another ten degrees, and he would have permanent damage. It was just a matter of time now.

𒀭

Calager and Sara were approaching the last known coordinates of Salaam. Sara could see the rise ahead but did not know that on the other side was a deep crater. Despite all the satellite coverage they had previously, the entire surface of Psyche had not yet been mapped. She only had the detailed maps that Salaam would complete on excursions across the landscape. Their speed had decreased slightly upon approaching the rise, but realizing their situation too late, Sara could not brake fast enough before they were airborne, sailing high across the crater floor.

𒀭

Flowing in and out of consciousness, Salaam barely had time to become aware of his condition. As he slowly awoke again, he could scarcely hear the wailing alarms in his suit, and it barely registered in his mind that the temperature read 116F. His vision was foggy out of his helmet glass. It was the last attempt of his body to cool down, expelling everything it had to his skin, to no avail. As he began to drift off, he floated past something odd on the face of the fissure wall. His last thoughts were of geometric lines as he lost consciousness altogether.

Sara panicked, knowing there was no way to return to the surface based on their current momentum and trajectory. Calager knew otherwise, and his space ops training kicked in. Nobody would ever plan to be in their current predicament unless they were trying to avoid an attack and needed a bit of sky. "Sara, we have but one chance to get down. Expel the topside O_2 tanks, now!"

"Sir, what in the hell are you talking about? There is no way to do that without cutting this whole life-saving mission short. We will not have enough to get back!"

"Sara, wake up, lady. Do you think we will do any better out in the blackness of space? Do it! He will have it! I know he will!"

"You are putting way too much faith in Mr. Dreamer. We just better hope he grabbed his suit and not someone else's."

Sara reached over to her left side and blew the valve as the O_2 jettisoned out the top side nozzles of the rover. The force rocketed them back down to the surface. This time Sara was ready for the approaching crater floor. She kicked the wheels into motion, hoping some forward velocity would lessen the vertical impact on the rover's shocks as they landed. They slammed into the ground with their helmets bouncing around like pool balls inside the rover. Calager's helmet hit her across the forehead, cutting a deep gash and allowing blood to pour down across her vision. She only saw it when she wiped her eyes at the last moment – the fissure opening.

Deep into dreamland, Salaam had not awakened again. His brain was shutting down. As he dreamed, he could see lines and geometric figures. Stone tablets written in the ancient Babylonian language of Akkadian were floating around him. He attempted to grasp them, but they floated just out of reach. Then he could see it – Jupiter growing in brightness from above. A smile spread across Salaam's face as he continued to dream. As the planet became brighter and brighter in the sky above him, he could see the ancient astronomers of Babylon calculating its position in the sky some 1400 years before anyone in 14th-century Europe. Jupiter's light blazed above him as his suit screamed at him, and the temperature rose to 120F.

Credit: Henry Sipes

From the moment the rover had hit the crater floor, Calager had been in motion. While his helmet collided with Sara, he was already in the back of the rover donning his rocket pack. When they had blown the oxygen tanks, his eyes had gazed below at the three boulders arranged in a perfect line. Before he could vocalize his thoughts, his training had taken over. He knew immediately where Salaam was. He turned around, picked up his helmet with Sara's blood dripping down the side, and locked it on his head. "You might want to put something on that cut. I mean, I've got blood all over my helmet."

Sara did not have time to take care of her cut as protocol called for her to lock her helmet on and assist Calager with his. Airlocks on rovers tended to be tricky at times. "Calager McGeen, what in the name of God are you doing?" Calager was diving into the airlock and engaging the systems. He just tapped his helmet to signal Sara to turn her helmet comms on. She never stopped yelling at Calager while fumbling to turn her system on. "….you sorry son of a gun, when I get my hands on you…what do you think you are doing…."

"No time to explain, Sara, and I love you too. Now turn the rover around and be ready to haul ass back to base when I return." Calager reached the fissure's edge and kicked off to force himself into the crevice as he engaged his rocket pack. *This is crazy, absolutely crazy, Calager.* He knew this was a wild idea, but he had to try. It would take all the fuel in the pack to pull it off.

Jupiter became a blazing sun in Salaam's eyes, and he absently raised his hands to block the searing light. It had no effect, and the pain became unbearable. Salaam began to panic, thrashing his arms and legs. He struggled to break free from the dream as his brain tried one last time to save itself. Allah was calling him home. "Salaam, my son, take my hand. You are home."

Calager reversed his rockets when he saw Salaam's suit come into view, slowing his approach until he floated beside Salaam. Salaam's arms and legs were pounding his suit as Calager tried to lock the cable to him. "Salaam, Salaam, wake up my boy! We're going to take you home, son!" Calager glanced at the temp readout and knew Salaam would not be waking up anytime soon. He attached the cable, flipped his orientation, and blasted the rockets to take Salaam and himself to the surface above. Calager was too busy adjusting their path to avoid collision with the fissure walls to notice the lines. No sooner than he had pulled Salaam over the top of the fissure, it slammed closed, and the regolith ever so slowly covered any sign it existed.

Doing a quick check of the back of Salaam's suit, Calager let out a big sigh of relief. *Thank God, Salaam; at least you remembered to actually pull the correct suit off the rack this time.* Calager had admonished Salaam in the past for running his oxygen tanks too close to empty. In case Salaam forgot, Calager had strapped an extra tank on for good measure. If they all wore their suits back to base, they would have just enough oxygen to make it.

The sands were crunching beneath his feet as he traversed the surface of the dune. Salaam looked up at the scorching sun and knew he only had a few hours left before turning around and heading back. He was not supposed to be here, but he always snuck away to see the old city ruins of Babylon. His mother would scold him if she found out. It was worth it.

Deep in the ruins, he found an intact tablet showing the Babylonian map of the world. The British Museum had what they thought was the only tablet. The one they had on display was missing some lines from the symbol. The cuneiform text described some rather odd regions of the Earth with fantastical creatures. Salaam always dreamed the map was of some far-off world. Stepping foot in the city, he imagined what it must have been like more than 2700 years ago, and to be one of the astronomers, gazing up at the heavens, Salaam began to feel cold. Very cold.

"Calager, he is coming around!" Sara continued applying more ice packs, crunching the contents as the chemicals inside began to cool them. Salaam's core temperature was down to 105F now, but she was not taking any chances.

Approaching the med table, Calager calmly began speaking to Salaam. "Old boy, you had us scared. Salaam, are you in there?" He was gently rapping Salaam on the head as Sara gave him a scolding look. Calager and Salaam were great friends, and he knew Salaam had a sense of humor. Still, the concern on Sara's face… He took Salaam's hand and calmly called him again. "Salaam, wake up, buddy."

Salaam began muttering. "Lines, lines, lines, Babylonian…" Then he fell back to sleep.

As Sara and Calager attempted to wake Salaam, Calager's workstation kept downloading the helmet cam footage. With their backs turned, they could not see the three-dimensional lines displayed on the screen. Nor could they see the data from his laser alignment measurements. The odds of three boulders with the alignment pointing precisely towards a star were one million to one. The three-dimensional lines were a map, the complete Babylonian map of a world, showing what the old tablet could not. It was the data they had been searching for, a map to a far-off world - a planet in the Aldebaran system.

Chronicle II: Caves of Atlal Babil

The Beginning

The sun began to rise, with the regolith coming to life like a field of fireflies ready to take flight. Except these were no insects, these were reflections of the sunlight off metal-infused grains of regolith. The asteroid Psyche had been pounded by stray meteorites and rogue asteroids for millions of years.

Credit: Henry Sipes

It was theorized that perhaps Psyche was left over from the great bombardment that had occurred three billion years ago. Perhaps it was truly the core of a long-dead planet pulverized from that time. If one had an astute eye, even bits of gold could be seen shining brightly in the sun. They were not here for the gold. Something else far more valuable drove these explorers.

One more mile, just one more mile! You've got this, girl! Sara Lafeete had been crawling through the maintenance tunnels for over three hours. She had long passed the pleasantry of just perspiring; she was sweating profusely. Her mind was getting numb. Having trouble focusing on her work, she watched as the beads of sweat gathered to form small pools in the bottom of the tunnel.

The section in which she worked had been pressurized to a comfortable one atmosphere, like Earth. That was the only similarity. The air was stale, and one could almost taste the recycled gases. Sara was a very petite woman for her family line of the French blue class. Struggling to reach 4'5", she barely qualified for the mission. In fact, they had made special compensation for her and many of the EETs, ETs, as Commander Calager McGeen liked to jokingly call them. He stopped his jokes there. The Electromechanical Engineering Technologists had his utmost respect from the word go.

Sara Lafeete was also graced with a perky personality and a beauty that far surpassed the Yellow Archangels of the French Alps where she grew up. When sunlight graced her hair, many a man would pause as if she actually were an angel passing before their eyes. *I suppose that is what caught Calager's eye, at least before my father squashed that thought.* Sara shook herself from her slumber, shaking her body from head to toe with a few slaps to the face for good measure. *Come on, Sara! Come on! You cannot fall asleep here!*

There was a reason for not falling asleep in the maintenance tunnels. Time was against all the techs as they worked their trade. Due to the radiation, there was a limit to how many hours could be spent inside. The complete installation of all radiation shielding was still several months off. The shielding was for without and within. Cosmic radiation continually bombarded the asteroid Psyche from without, and the thorium within the core added its own touch to the cocktail of excited particles.

Sara's crew was reaching a point where they could test their designs. They were researching and developing an automated system to traverse the tunnels and make repairs in the future. The United Arab Emirates (UAE) had taken a shoot-first-aim-later approach for some of the craft designs. Calager's light humor was not lost on the ETs as they felt like extraterrestrials on a strange world trying to develop the impossible – an automated maintenance and repair system that could survive for millennia. Sara attached her last cable coupling to the wall of the tunnel and turned around to head back to the base. Half asleep, she missed the rat's nest of cables above her, awaiting attachment and activation. As she dove down the transfer tunnel to the bottom, she did not feel the wires catching the hooks on her pack for storing spare tools or the radio that got pulled from behind.

𒀭

Salaam Rahal sat in the reactor control room, admiring his work. The output of the reactor was far beyond his expectations. With a seemingly endless supply of thorium at the core of Psyche, they would have boundless energy for igniting the massive nuclear engine to propel their craft out of the Earth system and to their destination, the Aldebaran star system. He had doubts, as did all the base, but the tablet said it was there. The Babylonian map he had inadvertently discovered when falling into the fissure months back had shown them the way, a bright beacon calling them from beyond. The hope for humanity was bound up into the map most referred to now as the Babylonian Lines. There was still no explanation as to why the map was set as a relief in the wall of a fissure that only someone from the inside could see. Psyche offered up her secrets in bits and pieces.

The great beyond is a stretch. 65.2 light-years is a vast stretch. Could they not phone home from somewhere closer? Salaam was not one for passing up space travel, but he did not relish lying in a stasis chamber like a pickle in a jar for eons. The nuclear engines would have to have the specific impulse to fly like the wind or, in this case, blaze like photons through the vacuum of space. They knew they could not go above the speed of light, but nobody said they could not play on the horizon. *I've got you, Babe. I've got you, Babe… to make me feel all right.* Salaam was singing a tune to himself from the great Lucky Dube. He could not go around the world to find that woman to love in the song. Salaam had to travel out to the asteroid belt, and his woman, well, let's say the old girl had some thrust. *When we light this candle, we had all better be suited up and strapped in because Babe ain't playing around. Hmm, perhaps I should get more creative with her name.*

𒐚

"Left… left… left, right, left… left… left… left, right, left." Calager McGeen yelled the cadence as he trained the new recruits in what little fighting force the UAE allowed him. He would take all he could get. That was no casual flyby they had had from that satellite six months back. *Off course, my ass. Some suggested it was a research satellite headed for another asteroid in the belt and only used Psyche for a gravity assist. That was no mere puddle jumper, mind you. That was high-tech. I saw the energy readings. It was scanning our base with every known frequency. Off course… that was a spy satellite.*

Calager already had first-hand knowledge of the recruit capabilities before him. They were hardened men and women coming out of many tough corners of Earth. The march was a method he had devised to see who would stumble first in the unfamiliar gravity of Psyche. One of the recruits, *what was her name, Shada? Or Shodia, or hell, no matter.* "Shahda, watch your step over that rock. You trip, you float, and I need you all anchored to the ground."

"Yes, sir! And sir, it is Shaahida!"

Shaahida hesitated in correcting Commander McGeen. She was a true Emirati. Her lineage came straight out of the Al Bu Falah tribe. Her fellow recruits may not have been cognizant of this fact, but she knew the commander might be. Her tribe was one of the most powerful tribes in the United Arab Emirates going back to the 19th century. Here on this rock, she wanted no special favors. She had won her place here with hard work, long hours of study, and even more active training. Her heart warmed as she remembered her father's words. *Shaahida, Allah has blessed you with the beauty of knowledge and of strength. Witness your gifts and make me proud.*

With a look of indifference, Calager waved her off. He actually did care, and eventually, he would have all their names memorized and locked close to his heart. He cared more than most about those that served with him. Of Irish descent and not long from that island, Calager understood the difficulties of names. Some would call him McKeen, McKoon, and some would try McGoon, but they were not standing long after. He chuckled under his breath, remembering that one time their sub had docked in the secret bay off the island. A bit rough around the edges, one of those types had discovered they were a bit too big for their britches.

"Okay, folks, that is enough for today. Let's head to the airlock and get some chow. Ms. Shaahida, you are with me!" As the last one entered the airlock, a few stars above winked off and then on again.

𒐙

I've got to get moving. Come on, Sara, move your petunias! Sara had glanced at her rad readout and knew she had pushed it too far. Their training had covered this particular unit of radiation closely. Her trainers had driven home the point, letting the crew know their cells would be *radi*cally agitated if not altered with too many rads. She had some potassium iodide pills, and dry swallowed a couple. They would help, but looking at the time and the distance needed to reach the tunnel exit, there was no choice. *Sara Lafeete, you are going spelunking, girl! First, we call in our* *position to Calager as that is protocol.* She reached to pull her radio, and panic set in. It was not there.

Salaam ran another pass through the data spewing out of the computer, tracking the state of the thorium reactor. Everything seemed status quo. *Hmm, that is a bit odd. That should not be there!* Salaam asked his AI to run another pass through the data. Perhaps it was just some anomaly. There were no energy readings near Psyche that would spark his data. Unless… He remembered that time in Iraq when they had been experimenting with different reactor drives. His commander had admonished him for his carelessness. They had shielding to block all outside energy, but he had failed to leave his communication device in the office that day. He had been chasing his tail, trying to find the energy source, only to suddenly and embarrassingly discover it had been his tail. His device had still been in his back pocket.

He had usually been given the grunt work inside the reactor drives. At times, he had thought his superiors were hoping he would get radiation poisoning. Still, he had felt their respect regarding his knowledge of thorium. Even after all this time, the tribal divides existed in his home country. His dark black skin and his family's history were not always his best friend. Some would suggest he was a black Jew from the Hebrews that escaped Egypt. Finding someone with his dark skin from the Kurdistan region of Iraq was scarce.

"Salaam, the data is accurate. There is an energy source in orbit." said the AI.

Salaam immediately made the call to Calager.

Credit: Henry Sipes

Only a few of the ETs were familiar with the expanse of the lava tubes that they were using for the mechanical tunnel runs of the ship. They were beyond extensive and not necessarily random.

Lava tubes were typically formed by lava flows as they crusted over. Generally, there would be a main tube, and then several smaller tubes would form as the lava cooled. Everyone knew lava flowed downhill. That was the conundrum on Psyche. Astrogeologists theorized it was the core of a planet. Yet, it had features similar to the *surface* of many planets. The lava tube sizes and lengths did not match up with the very low gravity and topography of Psyche.

The tube Sara was using at her location was sealed off to prevent any air leakages. She knew, however, that there was no chance of that. She had explored many of the lava tubes off the beaten path. They were all sealed. Another odd thing was the symmetry of the passages. Sure, as she thought, there was some symmetry in nature. She knew the smaller tubes would be a result of flow in the same general direction. However, these lava tubes were oddly straight shafts.

Traversing the tube was easy peasy for Sara. She tossed her bright blond hair back, gathering it together, and sat her ponytail in place. *It's time to get dirty.* She knew she would now have to crawl for some of the passage. She had mapped about half of the tube and knew for certain there was a section that went straight back to base. It would save her 45 minutes and a whole bunch of rads. She knew she had already hit the 200 rad level. *If I get back to base in one piece, they will probably shoot me up with massive doses of*

potassium iodide and some of that Prussian Blue in a creative cocktail. My
insides will glow blue like those Smurfs from that old 1980s cartoon.

"Okay, Ms. Shaahida, show me what ya got!" Calager had
decided it was time to see if she was worth all the hype from the
rest of the troop.

"Yes, sir!"

"Shaahida, let's drop the formalities on the mat. Look at me
as an adversary trying to smash your skull."

She was apprehensive at this change in McGeen's demeanor.
Up to this point in their deployment to this God-forsaken gray
rock in the middle of nowhere, he had shown minimal
personality. Most of the recruits jokingly described him as "the
stone." It had nothing to do with his physique but his total lack
of any emotion except hard-ass. Shaahida herself had become
hardened by all the training. Her muscles rippled under her tan
skin, but she had something else she had hidden from McGeen.
Speed. Her name meant "to witness." And in some cases,
especially concerning fighting, she had put this to good use. This
was usually how she defeated her opponents again and again.
She would witness their weaknesses and then pounce with
lightning speed through the chink in their armor.

Here today, Shaahida was a bit cautious. Now may not have been the time or the place to play her cards. Hand-to-hand combat did require strength, but strength alone would not win a strike. The force may cause damage, but it was the speed that would break through the shield of the opponent's defense. Calager took the first opportunity to land a blow to her right jaw as she made a mental note that he was a southpaw. She would have a bruise there later that would cause her some embarrassment with her few friends in their fighting unit. Shaahida landed a few blows to Calager's midsection, but for the most part, they did absolutely nothing. Calager had a six-pack, like his nickname implied, of stone. When she lost her concentration, Calager pulled a maneuver she had not trained for, the Jarakae Fad Hang. *Crocodile sweeps its tail,* was the movement in the natural world. The swing hook kick impacted her head, dropping her to the mat with stars in her vision.

"Come on, Shaahida! Some witness you are. Have you not seen me pull this maneuver with Sara? She easily blocks it. Why are you holding back? Do you think they are going to hold back when they arrive? Do you think this is all just some game?" Calager was showing just a bit of his temper. "I've seen your secret; now unleash it! Fight, Shaahida! Fig–"

Credit: Henry Sipes

Before Calager could finish, Shaahida did unleash her secret. She faked a punch to his face while dropping down to land a sweeping kick to his legs. Calager recovered quickly, jumping back to his feet only to find Shaahida was no longer in front of him. She may have been fast, but one secret she normally kept locked away was her past training in Plyometrics. However, her sensei liked to refer to it as flyometrics. He had trained his students to literally appear to fly with ease as if practically floating in the air. The hops, jumps, bounds, and skips of the Plyometrics combined with the strength of Shaahida enabled her lightning-fast soar over Calager. Before he could even react, she jumped to climb up his back, hooked her leg around his neck, and used her momentum to rotate him and drop him face down on the mat. Blood soon flowed from his broken nose.

Before Calager could regain his feet, the intercom blasted. "Calager McGeen to control center. We have company!"

Shaahida reached her hand out and assisted Calager to his feet as he held his sleeve to his nose to stem the bleeding. "Shaahida, you just got a promotion to sergeant!"

Shaahida hid her smile, but her pride and joy were beaming inside.

𒉀𒐊

Sara suddenly realized this particular lava tube was not the one she had traversed in the past. It finally registered in her mind she had been going in the wrong direction for more than fifteen minutes. Looking at her map, she thought, *but where exactly did I make the wrong turn… perhaps back here, or was it here…*

Sara could see that there was no way to determine her direction, leaving her with one choice – call for help. *Oh yeah, that's right, we cannot call for help because we lost our radio. Calager will either kill me or hang this over my head for a century.* Thinking back to her days caving in the Alps and especially in the Caves of Aṭlāl Bābil, Sara realized the full gravity of her situation.

The Caves of Aṭlāl Bābil were hidden under the well-known Babylonian Euphrates tunnel. Known in the caving community as an elite spelunker, Sara had been invited to assist with exploring the caves with only one condition – complete and utter silence. She could never speak, write, or in any way, shape, or form, mention anything about the expedition, ever.

She wondered why this memory came to the forefront of her mind. Then it came to her like a breath of fresh air – or lack thereof. In most caves there was always an air current of some sort. Many spelunkers had been lost over the centuries, but a few survived because they could follow the air currents to find their way out. It was a test of their senses, to be sure. They had to feel the air on their skin.

The Caves of Aṭlāl Bābil had been sealed like the lava tube she was lost in now. In order to preserve the findings in the caves, they sealed all entrances. Each spelunker was required to take air tanks while exploring. *This lava tube is sealed as well. There is no air current. I have no air currents, and I have no radio, and obviously, I am beginning to feel the brain confusion of rad sickness. Woman, you are stuck!*

Over the years, Sara had suppressed the terrible ordeal experienced by the research team in the Caves of Aṭlāl Bābil. They had planned well for their exploration that day, each taking extra air tanks, water, and emergency food supplies. It had not been enough. As they had gone deeper into the caves following a new tunnel, there had been an earthquake, and the tunnel had collapsed behind them. As if that had not been enough, the tunnels ahead had begun to flood.

Now in the lava tubes on Psyche, she shuddered, thinking back to that day. They were lucky to have made it out alive. Sara's mind may have been confused, but that day reminded her of one other possibility. There was a fissure near her current location that opened like clockwork. If that fissure opened and closed with enough vibration... *Stop it, Sara! The structural integrity of these walls was checked. Nothing will come tumbling down! I've got to keep moving. But in which direction?*

Credit: Henry Sipes

"What is the issue, Salaam?" Calager, walking into the control room with Shaahida, was in command mode now. Blood still dripping from his nose, he held his shirt sleeve up to stop the flow.

"Sir, do you need to take care of that first?" Salaam knew his readings were correct, but there was no impending doom at the moment.

"Salaam! Report!"

"Okay, I've been monitoring the energy readouts of the reactor, and as you know, we have instruments set up to scan for anomalies, like possible leaks, power spikes, etcetera. Well, we have an anomaly, but it is not on Psyche."

"Where is this *anomaly* now, Salaam?"

"Here, sir. It is in orbit. The AI is tracking it now. It is a highly elliptical orbit, but our sensors are extremely sensitive, and we caught its heat signature as it fired thrusters for a gravity slingshot maneuver using Psyche's mass."

"Fired thrusters? Our instruments are that sensitive? How do we know it is not just a rock with a high albedo reflecting the sun?"

"Ah, sir, unless that rock can reflect sunlight at timed intervals that slow its momentum, it is a spacecraft."

"How long before it is close enough to concern us?"

"We have about two hours before it could present some *concern*, as you say."

Calager turned to Shaahida. "Sergeant, your first command. Prepare the platoon. We may see some action! Salaam, where is Sara? Should she not have returned from her work shift by now?"

"She just missed her scheduled check-in about five minutes before you entered. Some of the team has returned, stating they lost radio contact with her. I've checked, and she is out of contact. You know there are those unexplained dead spots in the lava tubes. I'm sure she went off exploring a side tube on her way back."

"Keep me apprised, Salaam. If she does not report in the next thirty minutes, we have problems. You cannot ping her location?"

"Ah, sir, if we cannot radio her, we cannot ping her."

"Okay, wise ass! Again, report in thirty minutes. Shaahida, do you not have someplace to be?" Calager practically knocked Shaahida down as he yanked her arm, pulling her towards the door. He was not in the mood. "I told you all they would come, but did anyone listen? No! You all just laughed that I was overly cautious." Calager realized his concern for Sara was raising his temperature. "Okay, sorry. As they say, cool heads prevail. Let's work the problem by the numbers. First, we get all our ETs back and debriefed for more information about Sara's probable location. Second, let's get ready for this spacecraft."

"Sir, based on what data we have at this point, the spacecraft is not large enough to carry anyone." Salaam did not want to irritate Calager more but wanted to relay as much information as possible to prepare him.

"Salaam, the Mayim Chayim do not need troops. If they have enough instrumentation on board, they will gather enough data to ascertain what we are doing. What if they have something more nefarious on board? Like something nuclear? Believe me, my friend, this is an imminent threat."

"How would this holy water cult even know about our mission, Calager?"

"There is no wall of secrecy, no wall *period*, that cannot be broken, Salaam."

𒀭𒑐

The fissure opened on schedule, releasing the heat from deep inside Psyche. The vibrations were felt across the asteroid, but like with earthquake waves, Sara's area felt more shock, being closer. She looked up at the ceiling overhead, praying nothing would come tumbling down. A song from her playbook came to mind. *Walls come tumbling down, tumbling down... Who sang that song?*

Hmm, was it Style Council or Debbie Gibson? I can barely hold a tune, but perhaps.

"Playbook, who sang, 'came tumbling down, tumbling down.'"

Sara's onboard music device responded, "Sara, you must be more specific. There are 3,309 lyrics with those words, 113 artists, and 50 albums."

Before Sara could get more specific, the walls around her shook violently, and one wall came tumbling down. Sara's vision grew cloudy as the dust was all around her. She began coughing and sputtering, trying to breathe. She reached into her suit and pulled out her oxygen cup as the dust settled. Instead of a pile of debris, she found a solid rock wall blocking her intended direction of travel. Another wall had opened to her right. She stumbled to her feet and began to follow the new path as she had no choice but to keep moving and try to find a way back to base.

Unbeknownst to Sara, her rad sensor was malfunctioning. She was already receiving a higher dose of radiation, affecting her thinking abilities. Her map was turned upside down and she was traveling down a side fork of the main tunnel not yet mapped. Her rad alarm was already beginning to wail in her head.

ᚼᛁᛁᛁ

Credit: Henry Sipes

"This is it? This is really all we have?" Shaahida stared at the device in disbelief. "You really intend for us to use this to shoot down some satellite in orbit? This is barely more than a potato gun my grandfather would have used down on the farm."

"Shaahida, the last thing I need is attitude. It works, and that is all that matters. You do not need explosive ordinance to launch it. If your aim is true, it only takes a projectile to take down a satellite. In this case, the AI handles that. It knows the mass we are sending and the force behind it. It will calculate the angle needed before we fire to intercept the satellite based on its current orbital trajectory. All you have to do is load the mass. Now go!"

"Okay, sir. If you say it works, I believe you. Hopefully, it does not fail like Gramps' old potato gun."

Calager gave Shaahida a look. "Sergeant, do not make me consider a replacement."

Static began emanating from the comm system, and Salaam's voice came through. "Commander McGeen, the ETs lost contact with Sara back in maintenance tunnel twelve. She was finishing up some wiring there before heading back. That fissure nearby just now opened and closed, sending some pretty hard tremors through that area. Still no radio contact."

Calager looked down and mentally calculated the time. The answer was dismal. She was out of time fifteen minutes back. She would be experiencing rad sickness, and if she did not return soon, there would be no return. *Damn, Sara, your timing is horrible.* Calager knew he could not return another ET to find her as their rad levels were already maxed. With the satellite coming to its perigee, he had to concentrate on the immediate danger at hand. Sara had gotten out of tight spots before in caves. He would have to hope Sara had a way out of this one.

Sara practically fell into the next tunnel, dropping to her knees, and then laid down to rest. She knew this might be her last trip through a cave. Clearing the sweat from her brow, she slowly looked around the tunnel. The typical rock walls embedded with metals were oddly different here. Pulling herself to a sitting position, she began to scan the entire area. A loud noise behind her startled her as the rock wall closed. At first she panicked that she was trapped but could see there were several connecting tunnels ahead.

The last thing a girl needs is a jump scare here. I have got to be close to losing consciousness. There is no way this is real. Closing rock walls be damned. I am not losing it here. No way! Sara continued to look around and scooted herself over to the wall on her left. Contrary to most of the walls in the lava tubes, this one had an odd coating. Sara reached up to clean it off and gasped as all of the substance was sucked into the wall. Before her was now a language she had studied years ago and had personally only seen once on a rock wall.

Salaam continued monitoring the thorium reactor output. *Calager and Shaahida can worry about this possible attack. If we lose the reactor, some flying robot will be the least of our worries.* All at once, his energy readings were spiking again; this time, there were two of them.

"Ah, Calager, slight issue here."

"Salaam, what is it now?"

"I have two more high-energy readings. AI shows they are following the orbital path of the first one. There was a hard spike from each as the sensors picked them up."

"Shaahida, begin a firing run on the second craft!"

"Sir, should we not worry about the closest target?"

"Do as you are told! The first is of no concern."

"But, sir, the first object has slowed!"

"Sergeant, firing sequence on the second object, now!"

There was no time for Calager to explain orbital mechanics. Though it had been one of the challenging classes at the university, he had at least retained some of the knowledge. The first object had already passed perigee, so naturally, it was slowing down. He was now more concerned with the other two spacecraft. The first must have been providing data to the other two for an attack run on their location. As they reached perigee, anything they sent towards the base would have the highest velocity.

"Oh shi…It is what I would do. Using the extra velocity coupled with any missile engine velocity would provide just that much more energy for an explosive impact on our location."

muttered Calager. "Shaahida, belay that command. This is a coordinated attack. Target all three with as many projectiles as you can!"

"Sir, I have only loaded ten. There is no way to fire more than one at a time in sequence."

"AI, pull my program, Calager Shotgun."

"Downloading now... downloaded."

"Now, Shaahida, now! Fire! Fire! Fire!"

It was not like pulling a trigger on a gun. There were no explosive ordinance involved, no big kick. It was rather a melodramatic event to fire the device. She pressed the button on the console. They nervously awaited as the tracking screen showed ten projectiles scattering to fly toward the three energy spikes.

Credit: Henry Sipes

Slowly absorbing what her eyes were conveying, Sara knew she was definitely losing her mind. There was no way; 412,025,639 kilometers away from Earth, there was Sumero-Akkadian Cuneiform written on the wall of some dead asteroid. Conscious enough to still remember to check her vitals, Sara looked down at her rad readings. The numbers showed 999. She knew that could not be correct, so she smacked the device, hoping to bring it to life. Nothing. *Well, that can only mean one thing. If I leave here in one piece with my hair intact, no more X-rays for me.* She actually smiled as she realized what that meant. No more of those square plastic pieces being shoved into her mouth. *Heck, with our new oral hygiene products, I can probably skip that robot dentist altogether.*

As she turned back to look at the writing on the wall, only a few symbols made any sense to her. Oddly, the lines beneath one character were not written in standard Sumero-Akkadian. *No way!* Sara jerked her head to the right, where the three tunnels intersected her position. Looking back at the wall again, it was right there in front of her, a map. There was an arrow pointing at one of the lines representing the tunnels. Above it was a symbol she thought she recognized.

Credit: Henry Sipes

She traced the symbol with her index finger, hoping the sensation would jog her memory. It was made up of funnel shapes. On the left side were two funnels with the cups on the left and the spouts pointing to the right. They were oriented horizontally as if pointing at the four figures on the right. The right side of the symbol had four funnels orientated vertically with the cups at the top. The spouts were considerably longer than the horizontal funnels and stretched the full height of the symbol. Sara traced the symbol until exhaustion took over, and she laid back on the floor.

ᚻ||||

The projectiles were manufactured out of the brightest white marble from Earth and polished to a high sheen. Those in the control room could not see it, but there were just enough photons reflecting off the surface so the AI could track them. She displayed the action unfolding in space using the data from the energy spikes and the trajectories of their *marbles*. Everyone in the room held their breath except Shaahida.

She kept muttering under her breath. "Marbles, we are using marbles to hit some target the size of a small car! Marbles, of all things. Marbles!"

Calager picked up on her ravings, turned around, and said, "Zip it, sergeant! Just wait! AI, can you ping the targets?"

"Ping?"

"Yes, like the sonar ping of a submarine?"

"Yes, but…"

"Just do it for an old submariner."

Calager missed the days of living and working on his old navy submarine. The mock battles of cat and mouse play in the deep sea was an absolute adrenaline rush. Blasting sound waves out at 235 decibels across the depths and getting a ping back sure made the sailors jump. There was no water or air, of course, in the space above Psyche, so the AI simulated the effect of blasting radar waves at the targets and projectiles. A smile crept across Calager's face, and he chuckled to himself, covering his mouth before anyone noticed.

Trying to concentrate on the meaning of the symbol was impossible. Sara kept remembering her Iraqi teacher continuously repeating the symbols they were studying, over and over infinitum. She had always struggled with languages beyond her native French. The romance languages had many cognates, which helped her a bit when traveling around Europe. In Iraq, away from her homeland, she had been lost with Cuneiform. Her teacher had offered dinner to the entire class at his residence to drive some of the symbols home. *That is it! That is it! That is it!*

Sara jumped to her feet with a shot of adrenaline. She now knew which way to take. Their home base on Psyche was considered to be the most obvious place to set up their colony. It was the most expansive lava tube discovered. Home.

The AI kept projecting the objects on the large screen of the control room and emulated the sound of submarine sonar pings as the projectile and the targets merged upon one another. Then loud static broke and only three pings remained. The AI was now only displaying the spacecraft approaching perigee, with three pings coming over the intercom in sequence.

Shaahida and Salaam just hung their heads, knowing they had failed to destroy the spacecraft. They continued to watch the blips of the targets on the screen, waiting for the base's destruction. Total silence gripped the control room, and they all respectfully accepted their fate.

Sara hobbled along with more pep in her step than before as she progressed down the tunnel toward what she prayed was indeed the immense cavern of their base. There was always that chance that this was not leading her home. All the possible scenarios of failure coursed through her brain. She shrugged them off. *If I am going to die, I am going to die. I'll be damned if I do not try!* She picked up speed as she let hope take over. She was practically running now and turned a corner in the tunnel. Then, she came to a sudden stop and just stared.

$$\text{ᚼ}ᛏᛏᛏᛏ$$

The screen was empty of the three spacecraft radar reflections. This could only mean their reflections were mixed with reflections of the terrain of Psyche.

The three spacecraft must still be on an attack run, screaming towards the base only feet above the terrain.

The AI's voice crackled with urgency, "Base, prepare for impact in five, four, three, two, one!"

At that instant, everyone was prepared to die. Then the slow pitter-patter sounds of a light rain began to trickle through from the base structure's outer walls. The sounds could only be small particles of the spacecraft as they rained down harmlessly upon the base.

Calager broke the tension in the room laughing and spoke, "Coffee, anyone?" Salaam and Shaahida stood in shock, staring hard at Calager. They began yelling at him.

"Coffee! You think it's coffee time!" Salaam yelled and looked at him with anger.

Shaahida joined in, "Impending doom, death, destruction, and coffee? Calager, wait until we hit the mat next time. I'm going to clock your skull!"

"Easy, sergeant, easy! Remember, I am your commanding officer. Many things on this mission have been *need to know.* No one here needed to know until now. Shaahida, those *marbles,* you called them, were modified at my suggestion. Each one had an explosive ordinance embedded at the center, undetectable by any scans. The static noise we heard was ten *marbles* exploding into thousands of metal shards scattering like the beads of a shotgun blast. The United Arab Emirates determined that in order to keep these under wraps and hidden from any criminal intentions, I was the only person in the know. I do apologize for the drama, but it was necessary."

Salaam and Shaahida just shook their heads and headed toward the exit of the control room. Shaahida turned to Salaam, speaking, "I am going to need something a bit stronger than coffee."

ЯⅡⅡ

Staring back at Sara was a rough rock wall all too similar to many she remembered from spelunking in the Alps. She had stopped sobbing, knowing there was no point. This was the end, literally. The lava tube tunnel had reached a dead end. No moving rock wall this time. She obviously had been hallucinating this whole time. Her mind was playing games on her, pulling up old memories from the past as her subconscious realized she was dying.

Somewhere deep down, she knew it. Ignorance was bliss, and her optimism was pushing her to retain some hope, some joy to ease the pain of dying. Her days of exploring the caves beneath the Euphrates had been some of the happiest in her life. She thought of Calager, reminiscing on the times they had had together. Anger erupted from within. She began screaming. "Calager, you son of a gun!" She continued screaming and began punching the jagged rock, slicing her hands, punching again and again with pure rage. She was not ready for death. Blood began to stream from her hands, and the pain became too much. Sara collapsed on the tunnel floor and passed out as her heartbeat began to slow and skip beats.

Credit: Henry Sipes

Calager looked at the time, and then it hit him. *Sara!* He collapsed into his chair, realizing the situation. "AI, any signals from Sara?"

"No, sir. It has been quite some time now. I am afraid –"

"Silence! I know!"

Memories of their times together came flooding back, and the guilt stormed through him like a raging flood. *I asked her to come. I begged her to come. I have killed the only person in the universe who loved and accepted me.* Calager laid his head down, lost in despair, unable to accept the loss.

"Commander, I must alert you to some vibrations that occurred during the countdown to impact. I believe something from those spacecraft hit close by. I've lost some of the extraneous readings that I was recording during the attack. We might have some damage control ahead of us."

"I said silence, AI!" Calager raised his hand to slam down on the kill button to end the AI's ramblings. He needed to be alone in his agony. A fraction of a second before he hit the button, he stopped and looked up at the AI's eye.

"Where were you detecting these readings?"

"In the direction of the wall on the far end of the control room, commander."

Calager ripped his chair out of the floor and raced to the wall. He began pounding the chair against the rock in rage until it shattered. *It's no use. Give it up, Calager, you know this is solid rock. But maybe…* Calager looked around for anything he could use to pound the wall. He glanced to the back wall, and there was his battering ram; they kept emergency support jacks there just in case of a ceiling collapse.

Sara had told Calager countless times about air pockets and random passages created by lava flows long ago. Not all of the walls were solid rock. Some of the walls had layers of pumice that were formed from explosive volcanic eruptions involving water and gas. *There is a chance. There is always a chance. Damn, if I am giving up!*

He continued pounding until he thought he felt something give. *It has to be!* Calager continued pounding on that section of wall with increased frenzy. Finally, the rock wall crumbled, and he could see Sara on the ground there. He fell beside her and tried everything to wake her to no avail. Frantically placing his ear on her chest, he heard nothing. He plugged his right ear with his finger to block out as much sound as possible and listened again. Nothing.

Finally, Calager's grief at the loss of his wife pulsed through him, and tears poured from his eyes like sheets of rain. Slowly through the wall of pain, one thought broke through like a dagger. *She would not give up on me. She would not!* He placed his ear on her chest again. *Wait!* There was a very faint, languid beat.

"AI, call the medics! Stat! Stat!"

Weeks later, Salaam, Shaahida, Sara, and Calager gathered for a few drinks in the crew lounge. The drama from weeks past was slowly fading away, and they enjoyed the returning peace on

Psyche. They all had questions for Calager, but it was Sara who asked them.

"Calager, I think you have some explaining to do. The map of our destination Salaam found a year or so back, the perfect symmetry of some of the lava tubes, the Sumero-Akkadian Cuneiform I discovered, and the perfect nozzle shape of the largest crater all lead to one question. We are not just turning this hunk of rock into a ship, are we? Are we trying to jumpstart some ancient starship?"

"Need to know, need to know!" Calager knew it was time that everyone was brought on board. "Yes, from what we have discovered based on research from the UAE on Earth and here on Psyche, this is an ancient civilization's starship. There is much knowledge to gain, but it all leads towards an ancient civilization somehow tied to Babylon, the Caves of Aṭlāl Bābil, and Salaam's Babylonian Lines map leading to our destination in the Aldebaran system."

$$\models\mid\mid\mid\mid$$

Sara had joined Calager on the observation deck overlooking the bleak landscape of boulders, craters, and rifts across Psyche. In some ways, there was beauty there. It reminded her of something her grandmother had spoken decades ago about the trees in winter missing their leaves. They were still beautiful, standing stark against the grey clouds. Sara reached and embraced Calager's hand, sharing the moment.

"Calager, if my father ever finds out that we reconnected and Salaam married us on this rock, he will send more of those satellites. One will have your name on it."

Calager pulled Sara close. "I think the old admiral has other things to worry about besides us. Cult or no cult, civilization as they know it is finished on Earth. The thousands we will take to the Aldebaran system is the last chance for humanity to survive. It is the closest system with enough water to repopulate. We will never know why that ancient civilization came to Earth and settled in Babylon, nor why they left guides pointing the way to Aldebaran. I think they knew Earth was a temporary haven. Luckily for us, we have a chance to survive in this universe."

Chronicle III: Chariots of the Babylonian Forge

Day One – a.m.

Shaahida held her platoon in tight formation as they initiated a tactical assault on the simulated base camp set up in some random crater chosen by McGeen. *The man is anything but random. There is a hidden reason here. For the life of me, I cannot discern his choice.* It seemed like any other crater on Psyche. Gray. Dark. Lackluster.

16 Psyche, as it was formally named for being the sixteenth minor planet discovered, was worth a fortune for its metal content. The astrogeologists described it as a minefield of discovery, a chance to explore what they theorized was the core of an ancient planet. Most corporations on Earth viewed it as a world of riches, firing up a new gold rush. The UAE (United Arab Emirates) knew the true history of the minor planet and its purpose. It lay hidden beneath the metallic rock surface. On Earth, the UAE referred to it as their forward outpost to explore the Trojan asteroid belt beyond. In secret, they planned a mission to take them far beyond the solar system.

Shaahida raised her right hand and gave the signal. Her second in command, Joaquin Gonzalez, took half of the platoon quietly down the dark side of the crater's rim, east of the camp. She signaled the rest to follow her down the west side of the dark rim as they moved down to flank the base camp. Her platoon had planned the perfect attack. They would be in total darkness until the last few dozen yards. Prior to this exercise, they had calculated the exact timing of when the sun's light would creep over the crater's rim to light up the base. At that precise moment, they would emerge from the darkness, firing their momentum cannons to destroy the base.

As both squads moved to the edge of darkness, Shaahida held her fist up, signaling them to freeze. They checked their helmet displays and watched as the minutes counted down.

The squads were moments from breaking free from the darkness to spring their attack. Shaahida was praying she had trained them well. There could be no false starts in battle. There was no penalty and a five-yard pushback. Only death awaited a false start in battle. She motioned her squad to raise their weapons at the two-minute mark. At the one-minute mark, she activated her weapon and prepared to fire. Suddenly, streaking across the crater from the far side was a beam of light that lit up her squads like a fireball. Crater ray.

Credit: @Dedi5un

Alarms began wailing across the platoon's comms, and dust plumes began erupting all around them as momentum weapons pummeled the regolith, just missing their positions but surrounding them with dust that would take an hour to settle. Shaahida just hung her head. *Calager! You old dog!*

His muscle fibers tore by the thousands as his arms, pecs, and shoulders strained to lift his weight off the mat. His obliques were ripping to prevent him from falling to the side. Oxygen struggled to reach his muscles. As a result, lactic acid built to levels he had not previously experienced. Sweat beaded up and dripped off his skin, leaving remnants of salt and a pungent stench in the air. Doing one-arm pushups on the left side and then seamlessly switching to the right was not an easy maneuver.

Calager McGeen had clicked the accelerator workout room up to 2gs – two times the gravitational force of the Earth – pushing his body beyond its normal limits. He was preparing to face off with an unknown adversary. Anyone attempting to thwart their efforts to complete their mission would encounter a force of men and women trained by a man quietly referred to by his team as the *Stone*; he was six feet and five inches of uncanny intelligence, speed, and strength. The UAE had hand-picked him to be the commander of their base on Psyche.

Walking over to the accelerator control panel, he turned off the accelerator and danced in the gravity of the asteroid Psyche. He began to perform ballet moves as he effortlessly bounced and leaped across the mat. He was training to face any possible eventuality. With Psyche's gravity being a small fraction of the Earth's, he would use the accelerator to strengthen his muscles and practice dance in the natural gravity of the asteroid to achieve total control of his body for any hand-to-hand combat.

As Calager danced across the mat, he played back memories of a nightclub he had visited on leave in Faslane, Scotland. David Guetta's "Titanium" was pulsing across the floor with hundreds of bodies all smashed together, rising and falling to the beat. Sia was belting out vocals that only Sia could.

Across the dance floor, there she was. A lady dancing with hair that appeared to be lit on fire, as gold as the brightest wheat fields at the peak of harvest time. She rose up and down as if in slow motion, her hair flowing as if in a breeze, setting those same fields in motion. Calager just stopped frozen in time. There was his reason for living. There was hope, innocence, and beauty. The lady's eyes slowly met his, and she appeared to float in the surreal mist pushed out across the floor by the foggers. He would swear to this day that for a moment, just a moment, they physically touched minds across that dance floor.

"Calager McGeen to the observation deck!" Ada belted out across the recreation room, wiping the memories from Calager's mind.

"Ada? Really? Did you have to blow my thoughts away?"

"Commander, you asked for the alert before Shaahida's team attacked."

"I know, I know. Coming."

Calager pulled back one more memory from that night. As the dance floor cleared, he approached the lady. "Lieutenant Calager McGeen, ma'am. May I have the honor of the next dance?"

"Provided you never call me ma'am again. Yes, Lieutenant. I am Sara Lafeete."

A frown jumped across Calager's face. "As in the daughter of Admiral Lafeete?"

"Tonight, I am just Sara, so drop the frown and make me move like the waters you part in the ocean, Calager. Dance with me like there will be no waters to part tomorrow!" Sara winked at him as another Sia tune, "Unstoppable," vibrated the floor to life once again. *God willing, we will be unstoppable. God willing.*

"Commander?"

"Coming, Ada, coming!"

Credit: @Dedi5un

Sara and Salaam Rahal were talking quietly, looking out the windows of the observation deck. They were unsure of their purpose there, but when the commander tells you to be somewhere, you be there.

Salaam had arrived straight from the reactor room, wearing his radiation coveralls and smelling ripe from the extra heat spewing out of the reactor. He had pulled up the sleeves of his coveralls, showing streaks of salt left across his black skin from his sweat.

"Salaam, you could use a bath." Sara had to step away from the affront to her nasal cavities.

"Sorry, my lady." Salaam performed a mock bow to Sara. "We still have some work to direct one hundred percent of the reactor's heat into our power storage units. Hey! I'm only on my second pair of coveralls today. There was a time when I would have soaked three pairs by now. You are not exactly in perfect form yourself."

She scoffed, looking down at the oil and grease on her electrical technologist uniform. "Some of us are still crawling around like ants in a maze, buddy!"

"Still fighting with Ada?"

"You might say that. Ms. Lovelace wants it perfect, not ninety percent, not ninety-nine percent, but perfect."

Calager entered the room as Sara finished. He looked her way. She knew that look and smiled inside. She still had him.

Calager looked away, embarrassed he was that easily read. "Status, Ada!"

"Unfolding now, commander. As you previously suggested, they missed it."

Salaam shuffled over to stand next to Sara and Calager. "Let me guess. We have gathered here for one of your teaching moments?"

Standing tall, Calager said, "Watch and learn, Salaam. Patience actually does have some virtuous qualities." With a broad frown, he then grumbled, "Ada, open comms."

"Communication is open, commander. They can hear you."

Calager cleared his throat. "Oh, Shaahida! Did you forget something? Like, maybe just a little something? Know the geology of the battlefield, active and inactive. Someone must do the research. The data is out there. Use it! Do you think Salaam just dives right into swimming amongst his radioactive slurry without due diligence? What about Sara when she initiates a new electrical conduit for the ship's control pathways? Does she blindly cross wires here and there?"

Calager turned over his shoulder, looking at Salaam and Sara, motioning their way as if Shaahida were in the room. He was upset and very animated. "Do you see, folks? This is why we train. This is why we check and cross-check. This total failure across the battlefield is why I am hard on all of you. Achieving perfection will be a matter of life or death. Failure to evacuate the reactor room can lead to death. That is why we drill, drill, drill. Failure to reach a mechanical collapse in our ship tunnels can be catastrophic, that is why we strive for pinpoint accuracy of the failure point. Failure to research the battlefield can lead to the death of your entire squadron."

Shaahida looked across the landscape towards their home base. Though she could not see it from the depths of the crater, she could feel the look of disappointment and condemnation coming from her commander. *I did check the geology. Every single satellite image, every single data point. But...* "Gonzalez, get your ass over here, now!"

Day one – p.m.

Calager sat stewing over his dinner, mumbling as he played with his potatoes. Sara knew what was eating at him, but she was uncertain how to approach the subject. *Perhaps a bit of light talk will do the trick. I have got to get this out of him. Our lives could depend on him having a clear mind. He must have the confidence to lead.*

"Ada has been pounding us over and over again to perfect the timing of the maintenance shuttles. I mean, we are pushing 90% perfection. The system can send a shuttle to any point of issue within fifty feet of its location."

Lost in his thoughts of the training attack, Calager was barely conscious of her words. Then something caught his attention. *Fifty feet? Fifty?*

"Sara, fifty feet is the difference between life and death! Fifty feet shy of an electrical fire could be disastrous for the entire ship." Calager continued raising his voice as he released the anger and guilt building inside him. His muscles were clenched in his arms, and his veins bulged as he slammed his fist down on the table, shearing off one of the bolts that held it in place.

Reaching over, Sara placed her hand on Calager's arm. Her touch could calm the lion inside. She could feel his muscles relax. Now was the time. "Calager, you have sharpened that platoon into a razor-sharp blade that, when called, will provide ninja-like stealth and speed. There is no better fighting force within one astronomical unit."

"Sara, we are the only fighting force within several astronomical units, or we had better be. One astronomical unit is not as long as it used to be with the new rockets."

"You know what I mean. They are the best and would thwart most units on Earth. If those units were on Psyche, your team would have the upper hand."

"Upper hand? There is no upper hand with mistakes. One mistake, it only takes one, and they are finished!"

"Calager, you only knew about the data because of Ada. You had her scouring all the satellite information for a week, looking for an edge, anything that would trip up Shaahida's team. It was only that last data stream from Earth that coincided with Ada's that revealed the crater ray."

A small grin curved his mouth. "It was ingenious, right? Well, I guess I better visit maintenance, get some hardware, and fix this table. Then it is time for a debrief."

Many commanders considered themselves above the rest. Menial work was beneath them and should be delegated to those they commanded. Calager took responsibility for his actions, and in doing so, those under his command would mirror him. Besides, as he knew, getting his hands dirty fixing something would relieve his built-up stress.

Shaahida and Joaquin sat on pins and needles in the sparsely furnished conference room, fiddling with their fingers, looking down, and picking at old scabs from past training injuries. They were trying to think about something other than the stoic force about to enter the room, to no avail. Shaahida's disappointment in herself was palpable. She thought back to when she had bested McGeen on the fighting mat and realized she had let her pride get the best of her.

"Gonzalez, how many times did I tell you to scour all the data in the vault about that crater? How many times?" She was taking out her own pain and guilt on Joaquin, hoping to lift the darkness from her own heart. "You are the first to represent your country. The pride of Chile is resting on your shoulders. Is this how you want Chile's first astronaut to be painted in our jacked media feeds?"

"Ten times, sarge, ten times. It is my fault. I will take the blame." Joaquin did not know what else to say. He had already apologized numerous times since the exercise. He beat himself up for missing the crater ray. *It was not there. I looked. How could I have missed it? Abuelo, I swear I will do better.* Joaquin's abuelo, his grandfather, had barely survived the cruel dictatorship of Augusto Pinochet. As a teenager, his grandfather had escaped Santiago to work the fields near the small town of Bollenar. He had trained as a pilot at the local Santa Teresa airport and learned to spray the fields for pests. The flying took off and became a family business passed down to Joaquin's generation. Joaquin had no intention of flying crop dusters, though. He set his ambitions much higher and far beyond the atmosphere of the Earth.

The door to the room opened as if a boulder had collided with the frame. The doorknob practically ripped off as Calager entered. *Okay, maybe I overdid that a bit. Just a bit. I have got to remember that as their commander I want them to respect me not fear me.* Shaahida and Joaquin stood ram hard to attention with stares dead ahead. Calager sat down hard, stressing the chair's plastic legs as they bowed out and struggled to return to their upright position. He placed his fists hard down on the table, bouncing Joaquin and Shaahida's electronic training pads onto the floor.

It had the effect he intended. Shaahida and Joaquin were beginning to show more stress. One bead of sweat began forming on Shaahida's tan brow. Joaquin was becoming pale in the face. *Calager, enough, enough.* He could hear Sara's voice in his head calming him down. Perhaps he could show them a crack in the *Stone*.

"At ease. At ease. Take a seat." Calager motioned them down to the table. "Mistakes, mistakes, mistakes, we continue to make them time and time again. Report, sergeant!"

Joaquin began to speak up, "Sir, I am to bla—"

Shaahida placed her hand on Joaquin's shoulder. "Joaquin, we may all be to blame for this mistake. However, it is ultimately my responsibility. I was in command of the mission. The failure is on me. Commander McGeen, we had researched the landscape in detail, but the crater ray event was just plain missed."

Calager took in a deep breath as his massive chest rose and fell slowly. He let it out to ease his tension and the tension in the room. "Look, we are going to make mistakes. I am not worried about the mistake but the recovery and the lesson learned. The data was there, but it was not an easy find. I used Ada and some recent intel from Earth to find the perfect crater with a rim canyon that would create a crater ray. The lesson here for you is to use all available resources to your advantage. Use the AI, use recent data from Earth, hell, even use Salaam. He is always wandering around God's grey asteroid, getting lost in all kinds of crevasses."

Shaahida remembered the story about Salaam. One evening at the bar, when McGeen and the platoon were socializing in a more relaxed setting, McGeen had relayed the event. It was touch and go, with McGeen and Sara risking their lives to find Salaam. Salaam, himself, was not faring well as he floated deep down towards the core of Psyche in that fissure. She could sense a bit of humor in McGeen's voice now as he remembered that day. Perhaps the *Stone* was human, after all.

"Commander McGeen, I can promise you, it will not happen again!"

The far side of Psyche

Lance was not one to smile, not even a smirk. As he listened to the recorded communications between the base and the participants in the mock attack, a broad smile crossed his face for just a moment. He had his own data gleaned from reports stolen from the UAE. Members of the Mayim Chayim had given their lives to obtain the information. With the data and some other information obtained from Earth's largest telescopes, they had timed every single crater ray that would be to their advantage.

Lance had timed his landing to coincide with the crater ray to distract from the light of his rockets firing to slow his descent. Reaching up to his control screen, he pushed the power down button, and his craft went dark. He made a mental note to compliment the programmers of his spacecraft's navigation unit. Not only did they time his approach perfectly, but they also nailed the coordinates for his landing. His craft was buried deep inside the darkest crater on Psyche. Where his craft rested, the sun's rays would never reach. The crater's rim overhung his craft just enough to hide it from any satellite view. He was undetectable by any means.

Day two – a.m.

The lava tube was narrowing as they progressed. Sara had finally convinced Salaam to take a stroll beneath the surface of their home instead of gallivanting all over the surface. It took some convincing and some tricky manipulation, but it worked. As they progressed, the tube began to take on an odd shape. It was as if the random path of the lava that transgressed upon the ancient rock had been fighting against the gravity of Psyche. What they were traversing no longer presented a wide, rough-hewn path with a very low ceiling but a somewhat cylindrical tunnel with smoother walls.

"You were not kidding. I thought, perhaps the remnants of emotions from your ordeal had left your memory somewhat construed." Salaam was amazed at the transformation of the tube.

"Doubted me, huh? I may have been in a tight spot at the end, but my memories from before were not twisted by my radiation poisoning. I knew it was real. The tunnel's shape, that is. The Sumerian cuneiform symbols I found were also very real. Anything after that could be figments of my imagination. But Salaam, if this is truly an ancient civilization's ship, perhaps, just perhaps, the other symbols I imagined were real as well."

"Well, even if they were fake, this hike beats having to wear a suit, smelling a cocktail of sweat, plastic outgassing, and stale air. Though the air is a bit stale down here, at times, I get a whiff of something else."

Sara punched Salaam in the arm. "Okay, fine, yes, I saved a bit of deodorant for cases just like this. The rest of the base may have run out of aluminum zirconium tetrachlorohydrex gly, but not I."

"Tetrachloro what?"

"Oh, Salaam, you really do spend too much time down in that reactor. It is the primary chemical that keeps your underarms from spewing out stink. And no, it does not cause Alzheimer's. That was a myth. Ow!"

"Problems?"

"I just kicked something hard with my shin. Darn, that is going to smart!" Sara looked down and discovered the cause of the assault on her nerves.

"This is a rather odd shape for a rock. A rather odd shape indeed." She looked down the tube path, and not far away was another. Emanating upwards from both *rocks* was an arch that connected at the apex.

Credit: @Dedi5un

"Sara, I've seen something similar to this. I thought it was just my mind wanting to see something. Remember the video from my suit taken as I floated down that fissure? The map we found, those Babylonian lines, was on the rock face to my left. I swear there was something like this in the shadows of that video." Salaam reached up with an excavation brush he had brought along and began lightly dusting off the arch's apex. He gasped at what was hidden on the keystone.

The far side of Psyche

The light was beginning to fade as Psyche slowly rotated on its axis. As the last few rays of sun left the crater in total darkness, he began to prepare to disembark. Using the latest camouflage tech, Lance's rover was nearly undetectable. In the total darkness of Psyche, it would take an extremely sensitive infrared device to detect any heat signature.

It puzzled him why his employer took the name Mayim Chayim. *Living water?* Nothing was living about their organization. They barely gave Lance enough of their precious water to survive on this mission. *Well, they pay the bills. If I get off this rock, I'm set for life.*

Lance glanced up one more time at the stars above the surface of Psyche and watched as the UAE's satellite passed beyond the horizon. Firing up the rover drive, he checked the payload bay readouts. The device was there, a sleeping dragon ready to be awakened to breathe fire upon its prey. He ran some diagnostics on the armaments of his rover and began his ascent out of the crater.

"Good morning, Ada."

"Good morning, commander. Are you ready for the morning report?"

"Yes, ma'am. By the numbers, please."

"Sir, you know I am neither a female nor a male. Your programmers may have picked a name, but I have no sex."

"Ada, we have been through this before. Your namesake was Ada Lovelace, and she was a mathematical genius who happened to be female. Therefore, we think of you as female. Now, let us get on with it."

"Yes, sir. By the numbers, sir. First, all power levels throughout the base are nominal. There have been some occasional jumps in the reactor energy levels. Per Salaam, these may be normal. All systems completed on the ship are running, but not near the optimized levels I would like. Also, I will remind you that I still do not have access to everything. Our navigation and surveillance satellite reported a blooming event of the CCD camera. It appears the program mistakenly directed the camera toward a sun reflection off one of the highly metallic crater rims. Images taken after the sun event showed nothing unusual to report. Joaquin Gonzalez reported to the clinic for some facial abrasions. The report will show blunt force contact with something leather."

Calager looked up at that with an eyebrow raised. "Blunt force contact with something leather? Care to elaborate on that one?"

"Sir, I was told what happens on the mat stays on the mat."

"Yes, yes, you are correct. That was my command code." Calager could visualize what blunt force contact meant. It could only mean Shaahida had dropped Joaquin to the deck in training. None had bested her yet in simulated combat.

Credit: @Dedi5un

"Okay, Ada, I think that covers it. When Salaam and Sara get back from their spelunking trip, I will have him check on those reactor readings. Give Sara's team another six months or so, and all systems will be online."

"Yes, sir."

"Oh, Ada, send those CCD images to my console. I did a little CCD imaging back in the day. I'd like to tinker with that data. It could be useful for another training exercise. Did we catch anything on the radio spectrum when that event occurred?"

"I will send the optical data along with the radio, sir, though I see nothing outside of the typical noise from the metal surface on the radio image."

𒀭𒐊

Joaquin slouched in the corner of the mess hall, playing with his oatmeal. After the fight with Shaahida last evening, it was about the only thing he could get in his mouth. His lips were so swollen he had to force the spoon through. Half the contents would catch and drip down his cheek. He just gave up and threw his spoon down on the table. *The one day Chef has real blueberries, and I cannot eat them.*

"Having some trouble there, Corporal Gonzalez?" Shaahida had noticed him stewing and, instead of boasting, came over to cheer him up.

"Trouble? No trouble, sarge. I've got this." Joaquin tried his hardest to force his lips open enough for one more spoonful with no luck. For his effort, one of his bandages popped up, and blood began creeping down his face.

"Listen, Gonzalez. You left your guard open. I had to take advantage. It is the only way you will get better. McGeen says we have to take every advantage we can get. You left yourself wide open. I could have shoved a Mac truck through it."

"Yeah, sarge, whatever. Whatever you say, boss."

Shaahida stood to leave and turned back around, thinking about something McGeen had mentioned. *Shaahida, do not beat a man when he is down. Raise him up to fight another day, and he will fight with you, not against you.* "Joaquin, I may have taken advantage, but I've got some sore ribs this morning. You got in some good hits before then. Remember, it is not all about strength. Speed is essential to land the hit. Your strength is improving, but speed rules. Keep up the work in the accelerator. Now, where are those blueberries?"

Before Joaquin could answer, Calager walked up. "Corporal Gonzalez, do I remember your record showing you performed some image processing work back at the Extremely Large Telescope in the Atacama Desert of Chile?"

Joaquin was rushing to stand at attention when the entire bowl of oatmeal went flying, with blueberries hitting Calager's shirt. "At ease, corporal, at ease. Man, this is the mess hall. There is no saluting here. You know I gave the order that mess hall is your time to relax. Now, did you handle image processing or not?"

Joaquin very carefully reached over and removed the blueberries from Calager's shirt. "Yes, sir. I spent almost a year analyzing data at the observatory complex."

"Great. Now get cleaned up and meet me in the control room at oh-nine hundred. I've got something I need you to take a look at."

The far side of Psyche

The sidearm lay beside him as if an extension of his arm. The weapon was sparkly clean, yet it still had the rich, musty smell of gunpowder. He could even see smoke rising from the barrel and feel the heat from the muzzle. It was all just memories of a tool that was a means to an end.

He cared not if a launch facility later detected evidence of explosive ordinance. This was his weapon of choice, and he was going to use it. On the grip were nine scratches, all equally spaced apart. *Nine kills for the cause. Calager McGeen, my friend, you will be number ten. The Mayim Chayim have spoken, and your water will be added to theirs.*

Lance reached over and powered down the rover for another rest period. He would sleep when the sun covered his side of Psyche and awake again as the darkness approached, and watchful orbital eyes had difficulty detecting his movements.

𒀭𒐉

Salaam continued brushing off the dust from the rest of the arch keystone, revealing cuneiform symbols littered over the surface. "Sara, if I'm not mistaken, you have some knowledge of these."

"I am most definitely not an expert here, Salaam. We found these same symbols deep in the Caves of Aṭlāl Bābil. Oh, shoot, I am not supposed to discuss that with anyone."

"Sara, we are several astronomical units from Earth on an asteroid that now appears to be much more than some metallic space rock, and you want to keep information from me?"

"Okay, okay, brush off the rest of this, and let me step back and see the whole picture."

Brushing off the entire arch, at least twelve large symbols revealed themselves. Down near the arch on both sides were rocks that had dust crusted on their surface. Salaam pulled a rock pick from his pack and began to chip away at the debris. Then, at once, the debris cracked like the shell of an egg, breaking off to reveal a perfect cube of some unknown metal.

Credit: @Dedi5un

"Ah, Sara, these are not rocks. If I had to guess, these might be some type of power cells. Any luck with those symbols?"

"My memory is a bit foggy from our time in the caves. The language expert was lost during that particular journey. Look at this symbol here." Sara pointed to one of the symbols near the left of the keystone. "That symbol would seem to represent something like a chair in English. The other symbol on the right is… no, that makes no sense. I would have thought it meant to fly. Sorry, Salaam, this is not my area of expertise." Sara absent-mindedly pushed the symbol that was at waist level. "Now, this one, I know. It means to open."

Suddenly, the cubes at the base of the arch began to glow.

"Power cells, I knew it!" Salaam was excited that his guess was correct.

The power cells glowed brighter, and a rumbling noise began inside the rock wall. The archway began to vibrate, shaking as if an earthquake was disturbing its slumber. A loud scraping noise like sandpaper on rock began, and the arch opened, expelling a stagnant air filled with dust. Salaam and Sara began coughing and immediately donned their oxygen masks.

Beyond the arch was a massive chamber that went on as far as the eye could see. Stones along the ceiling began to glow in sequence. One by one, metallic objects began to rise off the floor and hover silently. A line of lights on the floor shot out into the distance like the runway lights of the old airports on Earth.

"Salaam, the symbols meant flying chariots. Wait until Calager sees this."

"Are you sure, Joaquin? That could just be a spike in noise in that section of the chip." Calager was not convinced by Joaquin's analysis.

"Sir, I've subtracted thirty to forty dark images of just the electronic noise, and we have looked at numerous other images taken. That is not noise, and it is not a hot cell on the CCD chip. There was something at that location emitting energy."

"Joaquin, that is a dead crater. There is nothing there. Unless…" Calager reached over and hit the intercom button. "Shaahida to command. Shaahida to command. Now!"

Shaahida grumbled as she was shaken from her morning meditation. It was a practice her sensei had ingrained in her to center her thoughts. She would become one with herself and expel the old fears of inadequacy from her youth. *McGeen, you had to break up my morning routine now?*

She sprung off the floor from her crossed-leg position and blew out the candle. An open-flame candle was, of course, not allowed on base, but she had disabled the sensors in her quarters. As a precaution, she did have an oxygen depletion device nearby. *Okay, McGeen, I'm coming.* She threw on her uniform and headed out the door.

The far side of Psyche

Darkness descended upon the crater, providing Lance with a cloak to conceal his coming onslaught of destruction. The

Mayim Chayim had given him two tasks. Destroy the base and guarantee Commander Calager McGeen dies. The device would take care of the base, but he needed Calager out in the open. He needed to see Calager die by his hand.

That should do the trick. One more emission like that, and he will come. Lance pulled up his navigation map and double-checked the crater where he would entice Calager to search. He knew others would come. The Mayim Chayim may have cultivated themselves as the living water saviors of the Earth, but the depths they would go to for their survival were limitless. They would sell their souls for their cause. The weapons they designed for his rover were unique in their destruction.

𒀀𒑊

"Sara, you can call it in, but we must check this out. We can leave our backpacks here in the doorway in case a mechanism or power failure closes the door." Salaam was chomping at the bit to go exploring.

"It is too risky, Salaam. What if something happens to us while we are inside, and they cannot get to us in time?" Sara had a very good reason for being hesitant. Being lost in the lava tubes in the past, running into a dead end with radiation poison to boot, gave her an extra appreciation for danger within the maze.

"Okay, how about this. We leave both backpacks in the doorway, and I go inside, only far enough to get some energy readings. I will always stay within visual contact."

Sara considered all the possible scenarios of doom and decided Salaam's proposal to be minimal risk. "Okay, but I'm calling base to alert them of the excursion. Lafeete to base. Lafeete to base."

"Ms. Lafeete, base here, how can I be of assistance?" Calager had the AI programmed to handle all communication with work teams in the extreme case that no humans could reply. It was an afterthought following Sara's collapse in the lava tubes many months back. Everyone had a communication device sewn into their uniforms. He swore no one would ever be out of contact because of something as accidental as a dropped radio.

"Ada, please alert the commander. Salaam is going to investigate a large cavern that has just opened up beyond our location. We have taken precautions in case the rock wall attempts to close. Ada, can you monitor our view screens and record everything?"

"Yes, Ms. Lafeete, I will contact the commander and record audio and visual. Ah, Sara, I do not mean to infringe upon the privacy of teams away from the base, but at times I do monitor your activities. I do not want to lose anyone off the radar again.

There are energy readings in that cavern that are not in my database. Please proceed with caution."

What is it with everyone? I do not need to be pampered. My situation could have happened to anyone, anywhere. This is a space rock. "Okay, Ada, we will proceed with *caution*."

𒐖

Ada had been monitoring the discussions between Joaquin and Calager as she ran her data analysis. She noted that more images of the surface had come in overnight. "Gentlemen, I have another set of data coming in. There appears to be another energy spike closer to base now, in the Achilles crater."

Shaahida walked through the door to command and control as Ada finished. Calager looked up from the console as she approached. In a rush, Shaahida had not quite finished straightening her wardrobe to his satisfaction. "Did you sleep in that uniform, sergeant?"

"Sir, I was in the middle of meditation when you called. You sounded concerned, so I rushed. This is not a dress your best time, right? No fancy tea, right?"

"Testy, testy, testy, are we? Take a breather, Shaahida. You need to recognize a little light-hearted ribbing when it is not a condemnation." *Hmm, perhaps I need to work on my tone inflections. I need to come off as a commander who commands respect, but I also need the team to want to respect me.*

"Let's try this again, shall we? Good day, Shaahida. Thanks for joining us at such short notice. I know your meditation is important, but we discovered an odd energy reading on some images of craters several clicks beyond the base. Ada just confirmed that we have another in Achilles. I am not one to believe in coincidences. Bring your platoon to combat alert status immediately."

"Sir, we have had energy readings before. They have always been some bright metal on the surface reflecting the sun's rays just right."

"True, Shaahida, but these energy readings form a straight line towards our base. Adversary or fluke, prepare the platoon. We leave at thirteen hundred. I will command the expeditionary force. I need you to pull up all tactical assault data we have for that crater. And Shaahida, pull all the sun data this time. Joaquin, you will stay here at the base with two squads. If this is a fluke of light, everyone gets a few weeks of downtime on me. If not... well, let's face that when it comes."

Shaahida and Joaquin snapped to attention, and their demeanor changed within seconds into battle mode.

The far side of Psyche

That should do it. If I know Calager, he will be coming with half his command. Using the benefits of the sun's rays at the highest angle across Achilles, Lance had hidden the Excalibur units across the crater.

The Mayim Chayim had stolen the design data from what was left of DARPA. It was mostly a mothballed organization now, but the US Defense Advanced Research Projects Agency had developed the units for action in space decades ago. Similar to the Gatlin guns the cavalry used in the old Wild West, the Excalibur devices could wreak havoc upon any advancing force. Only instead of firing bullets, the turrets fired lasers. The Mayim Chayim had taken the liberty of miniaturizing the devices further using new technology. They could be easily concealed now like the old mines outlawed by the Geneva Convention a century ago.

Now for my favorite toy. It was not lost on Lance why the Mayim Chayim had chosen this particular weapon. It was another design from DARPA that just coincidentally had a name very similar to the cult. MAHEM – Magneto Hydrodynamic Explosive Munition. The device would fire an explosive-driven chemically molten metal that would blast through any target. This particular unit had been optimized to bring any metal it came in contact with into a molten state.

He finished setting the device in place on the top of the central peak of Achilles. Many craters formed by massive meteorite impacts had central peaks. This particular one was almost perfectly formed with a plateau on top that offered not only a great launching point for the weapon but an easily defendable position. He finished covering the unit with camouflage and bounded back down the side of the crater, enjoying thoughts of the destruction to come.

Day two – p.m.

"Come on, Salaam, report! We are not spending the night in here." Sara understood Calager's communication protocol using Ada, but she would like to speak directly to her husband about this find. It was breathtaking technology buried deep in Psyche with no apparent purpose.

"Sara, I cannot put this into words. What I see here before me defies the laws of physics. From my initial analysis, this is… okay, do not laugh. This is a hanger of sorts. These are craft. There are hundreds here. It is eerie as there is absolutely no noise coming from them. They are simply floating."

"What would be your scientific opinion on their purpose?"

"If this really is some ancient spacecraft pretending to be an asteroid, these would be, in my limited understanding, defense units of some sort. But… why would a craft from another world need so many? Our world would have had zero space tech at the time they may have arrived. And these can only be used for surface defense."

The Achilles Crater

"I want our squads spread out as we approach Achilles. Shaahida, take the Alpha squad and flank to the left. I will take Bravo and flank right. Based on the sun data, we will have about thirty minutes before it lights up the central peak and several more before the crater rim on this side lights up.

"Roger, sir."

Shaahida and Calager separated their helmets from contact. They had been radio silent for an hour and would only communicate through the vibrations between their helmet visors. Shaahida and her squad left their rovers behind and began advancing up the crater's rim. Shaahida motioned her squad to spread out and stay low as they ascended the rim.

Standard safety protocol for spacewalks across Psyche required white suits, but her squad wore stealth operation suits cloaked in the latest light-absorbing material. Black did not even come close to describing them. No reflection of any kind could be seen. For Calager, it was always a bit disconcerting to see his troops just disappear.

He motioned his squad to ascend a click from Shaahida up the east side of the slope. *If Shaahida analyzed the geology data correctly, we should descend to the shadow on the other side in unison.* Calager checked the time on his heads-up display as he descended into the crater. Without seeing the rest of his unit, he could only rely on their training to assume they were all in place and spaced across the rim.

The sun's rays began to spread across the crater floor, creeping towards the central peak. Based on satellite data, this was the last known anomaly on the imaging scans.

𒐫

Where are you, my friend? I know you would not send out your people alone. Too proud to leave the fight to others! Respect? What about respecting your own to achieve their objectives? How about having some faith in your people? Lance reached down with his left hand and initiated the power sequence on the MAHEM. He pulled out his 9mm holstered on his right hip, carefully checking that he had chambered a bullet and his clip was full.

He crawled around the plateau, careful not to scrape his suit on anything sharp that may compromise the fabric, exposing him to the elements of the vacuum of Psyche. Having confirmed that each Excalibur was powered and scanning, he settled down and waited. *Oh, you knights of the dark, come to me. Running silent through the deep. Pray for your souls to survive the sea, do ye? Prepare yourselves to survive eternal sleep, for ye are mine to keep.*

He kept repeating an old poem that would play in his mind. He may have left the ocean's depths, but darkness had spread across his soul deep below. He was the killer whale, and they the seal, and oh, how he wanted to lunge to sink his teeth into their flesh. *That submarine would have imploded, killing a hundred souls, but old McGeen made us stand down. Not this time, McGeen. This time, they will bleed. You will bleed and face eternal sleep.*

"Ada, are you getting the recordings from Salaam's camera?", Sara questioned.

"Yes, Sara, all video and what little vibration I can detect is being recorded. Salaam may not be able to detect it, but there is a subsonic hum coming from those units now. Something has activated them."

"Ada, please patch me into Calager."

"Sara, at the moment, Calager and two squads are performing exercises near Achilles."

"What do you mean they are performing *exercises*? Why was I not informed?"

Ada did not want to alarm Sara. She knew there was nothing she and Salaam could do to help the situation. The probability of there being something nefarious near Achilles was pretty minimal, but she knew Calager would not let it go without checking it out. *What to say to Sara?*

"Sara, the commander wanted to perform live exercises with the squads. To their knowledge, this is not a drill."

"Squads, Ada? How many squads are out there? Who is in command of the base?"

"At the moment, Corporal Gonzalez."

"Get the corporal, Ada."

Ada pinged Joaquin, and he joined the conversation. "Corporal Gonzalez here, ma'am. How can I be of assistance?"

"Corporal, how many squads are you commanding?"

"Two, ma'am. McGeen has taken the rest for the exercise."

Sara knew that if this was truly an exercise, she could break in and speak directly with Calager. With the discovery before them deep below Psyche, she knew he would want to be notified.

"Ada, open a channel to Commander McGeen."

"Ms. Lafeete, that is not possible currently. Commander McGeen has requested complete radio silence. They have turned off all communications."

"Ada, open channel SL1 then." Sara was beginning to think something was up. Ada was now calling her by her last name, and Calager never went completely dark.

"Ms. Lafeete, all communication has been cut off. There will be no communication until the mission is complete, or –"

"Ada, I thought you said this was a training exercise? Calager never calls exercises missions. What is going on? Corporal?"

ﬤⅠⅠⅠⅠ

Shaahida checked the heads-up display and confirmed it was time. She knew her squad had spread out and was now searching for the cause of the energy reading. They had trained hundreds of times how to sneak up on an enemy without communications or line of sight with their fellow squad members. The walk was ingrained in their memory now. They could literally do it blindfolded.

She knew McGeen would be doing the same to her east. Her team had done their due diligence and knew the terrain down to every last boulder. Though on the crater floor, it was sparse cover. They would have to make do.

$$\vdash\!|\!|\!|\!|$$

Sensors began lighting up the screens on the Excalibur units. Lance knew the only way to detect an advancing unit of McGeen's was to install vibration sensors on the crater's floor. Coupled with these, he had installed infrared lasers crisscrossing the crater to determine the precise locations of any advancing trooper. A smile spread across his lips as the Excalibur units began firing hundreds of lasers across the crater. He pushed the launch button on the MAHEM and descended the peak to the north.

$$\vdash\!|\!|\!|\!|$$

Ada had been monitoring the exercise at Achilles and realized the worst was happening and called out. "Corporal Gonzalez, we have an issue."

Corporal Gonzalez stressed between satisfying Sara and the AI. "Sara, let me get back to you. Ada has some data to discuss."

"Joaquin, I had better hear back in five, or I am coming up there myself. Salaam, get moving. We need to leave," Sara pleaded with Joaquin and Salaam.

Salaam had gone far beyond what he and Sara had agreed upon. He had been following the long stretch of lights, curious about their destination in this deep cavern. *Well, this is a bit strange.* He had realized that the elevation was changing. As he followed the lights, the smooth floor had risen substantially. In the distance, he could see an immense arch with massive power units on the floor on both sides.

Salaam turned back around and headed out to meet Sara. All along the walls of the cavern were spacesuits with lights activating. *What? This cannot be.*

Credit: @Dedi5un

Blinding laser arcs were flashing all around Shaahida. Dust clouds exploded off the surface. Lasers were pulverizing the regolith further into tiny bits of debris as they were closing in on her position. She was trapped in a vice that would slowly squeeze the life out of her squad.

"Sergeant, I'm hit! I'm hit…" One of Shaahida's squad yelled out.

Shaahida turned to her right and stepped forward just as a bright beam crossed where she had been previously standing.

Another trooper yelled, "Losing pressure, can't plug the hole! Sergeant, help us!"

"Joe just lost his leg right in front of me! They are cutting us down like a knife through butter!" Screamed another soldier.

Shaahida knew if she did not act swiftly she would lose the rest of her unit. "Break formation, seek cover! Now! Drop flat to the ground, soldiers!" She could see the lasers firing from the central peak. "Concentrate all weapons on the peak! Fire! Fire! Fire!" She quickly checked her six and called Calager. "Sir, it's FUBAR here. I'm losing troops left and right."

Credit: @Dedi5un

"Hang in there, sergeant." Calager switched to an open channel and called out, "Pull your skivvies up and chill your suits soldiers. They have got to be using infrared sensors to hit us this accurately. Freeze in place until we can get some eyes in the sky. Ada, are you there?"

With the bright lasers melting rocks all around their positions, no one noticed the light leaving the peak and traveling south.

𒐉

Calager had dropped at the last minute behind what little cover he could find, a small boulder thrown from the original impact that formed the crater. He assumed a fetal position, pulling himself into a tight ball, barely having enough cover to protect his massive bulk. It was not a moment too soon as the lasers began slicing the darkness around him.

He bit his lip as memories of unit members flashed through his mind. This was a killing field that the best of soldiers could not survive. Hearing Shaahida rally her squad bolstered his faith in her selection as sergeant. *I'll be damned if we go down like this.* "Bravo squad, coordinate firepower with Alpha squad on the peak now!" Only static was heard as Bravo team did not reply.

Lance had fallen back to his rover just behind the north rim of the crater. He laughed as he filled up his suit's oxygen tank. He could hear the radio chatter across the crater floor as Shaahida's troops were dropped, screaming for help. It was just a matter of time. Then he heard the call he had been waiting for. *Ahh, there you are, my old friend!* Locking his helmet, he checked his seals, exited the rover's airlock, and pulled his weapon from its holster.

"Salaam, let's go! Run! Something is wrong. We can come back later to document the findings."

"Sara… you are not going to believe this!"

"Ms. Lafeete, Ada here."

"Ada, your voice is unmistakable. No need to announce your name. What now?" Sara's temper was firing on all four cylinders now. *Salaam is off on a lazy stroll, Ada has developed a personality complex, and Calager has gone off on a mission… a mission of all things… and does not bother to contact his wife. This cannot be good!*

"I am sending Corporal Gonzalez to your location."

"The last thing I need is some corporal coming down here to aid our egress, Ada. I've got enough on my hands with this wandering Salaam. Like, what the heck is going on?"

$$\vdash\!\text{TTTT}$$

Calager assumed the worst, with no reports coming in. He knew this was not some random assault. This was a trap. They were purposely drawn to this spot like pigs to slaughter. It would cost them later, but if he did not get some tactical advantage, they were all doomed to meet the cleaver today. *Where in the hell is Ada?*

"Ada, come in! McGeen to Ada! McGeen to Ada!"

"Yes, commander?"

"I need a redirect on the satellite to our location. ASAP. I need a full spectrum scan of this entire crater area, and I needed it yesterday."

"Sir, a redirect will cost too much fuel to continue operations later."

"Ada, there will be no later if we are all dead! Do you want to be alone on this rock for the rest of your powered existence?"

"Redirecting now, commander. Maximum thrust will bring it over your position in five minutes."

Knowing he was pinned down, Calager called out to Shaahida. "Sergeant, Bravo team is not reporting back. Continue your barrage on the peak until we can get more intel. I've got Ada bringing the satellite around to get eyes on this adversary. Give that peak all you got!"

"10-4 commander. What about you?" Shaahida yelled back as she fired round after round from her momentum cannon.

"Do not worry about me, sergeant. This old dog still has some bite left." Calager raised his weapon and risked firing off some shots at the central peak even as lasers melted chips out of the boulder where he took cover.

I've got you now, my friend. Getting sloppy in your old age. Lance double-checked the coordinates again and slowly made his way to Calager's hiding place. He adjusted the Excalibur units to open up a broad swath to allow him to approach without getting hit. Taking the safety off his 9mm, he effortlessly moved within yards of Calager's position.

Corporal Gonzalez and his squads rushed to Sara and Salaam's location solely on a guess from Ada. *A guess from an AI is good enough for me. Who am I to second guess the processing power of twenty supercomputers? She must know something.* Rounding the corner, he found Sara fuming mad about being left in the dark.

"Corporal, this had better be good. Report!"

"Ms. Lafeete, Ada directed my squads here with all due haste. I do not know why."

"You are following the commands of Ada without confirming with Commander McGeen? Have we lost all command protocols?"

"Ms. Lafeete, she seemed..."

"Sara and Joaquin, you have to listen to me. Our base and the squads at Achilles may well depend upon your following my lead." Ada's voice inflection had changed to get the importance across. "I need you to do exactly as I say."

"Ada, where is my satellite?" Calager yelled in desperation to Ada.

"Over your position now, commander. Scanning all electromagnetic frequencies. Sir, you have a signal at..."

"Yes, commander, you have an infrared heat signature right behind you." Lance stepped around the boulder Calager was using as a shield to block the lasers.

Calager knew that voice. He spun around, already firing his momentum cannon when Lance stopped him short with a shot to his abdomen. Calager had no choice but to drop his weapon and plug the hole in his suit.

Credit: @Dedi5un

"Ada, have you lost your circuits? You want us to jump on these things and fly where?" Even Corporal Gonzalez had his limits. He was starting to wonder if Ada's program was malfunctioning.

"Corporal, I have clear data now from the satellite at the Achilles crater. Commander McGeen's squad is dead, and half of Shaahida's squad is down as the result of a barrage of laser fire from the central peak. There is an extra heat signature not accounted for, and I am receiving radio signals from this unknown entity at the commander's location. Grab suits and get your squads on the chariots!"

"Ada, there are no controls on these things. How are we supposed to –"

"Corporal, your commander's life and the lives of everyone on this base depend on what you do next."

𒐊

"I bet that hurts." Lance just stood over Calager, laughing at getting the best of the great Calager McGeen.

"The old man sent you?" Calager grunted as blood began to fill his suit. He had no way to plug the hole in his abdomen. Thanks to some inventive engineers in the UAE, the goo was at least plugging his suit's holes for the moment. The bullet had gone through one side and out the other.

"Old man? That old man is now the leader of the Mayim Chayim."

"I did not think you the religious type, Lance."

"It all pays the same, McGeen. They may be a cult, but they have the means to pay. I could not pass up the chance of adding your notch to my gun." Lance glanced down at the read-out on his arm cam. "In a few more minutes, I will add a bunch of notches to my belt."

Sara and Salaam rushed to assist Joaquin with suiting up his squads and helped them climb aboard the chariots. Sara was astonished as the suits' membranes were warm to the touch and instantly morphed to encapsulate them in a tight symbiotic embrace with the chariots. Sara approached Joaquin's chariot. "Joaquin, it is up to you now. Godspeed."

Sara and Salaam turned around and ran to the arch, exiting just in time as the hangar wall opened with sunlight beaming through. At once, the chariots sped towards the opening. Three of Joaquin's squad, struggling with their suits' interfaces, bit the dust, losing balance and getting slammed into the floor. Joaquin glanced their way, struggling to remember their names. *Ada, I hope you know what you are doing, or there will be hell to pay. I will melt down your chips one by one.*

As Lance glanced down at his arm cam, Calager acted. He performed a perfect pirouette, launching himself over and behind Lance, grabbing the man by the helmet. Lance reacted just as fast, shooting Calager again, hitting him in the shoulder. Calager jerked back. He now had two holes to plug.

"We practiced in simulated Psyche gravity on Earth, buddy. Did you think we did not have the capability? You are just not that fast these days." With a smug smile, Lance raised his arm cam to show Calager. "See this dot? That will melt your entire base into sludge as you slowly bleed out."

"Sara is in the base, Lance!"

"Well, you will have to give her my regards, buddy. The old man said to finish every last one. I guess Admiral Lafeete has had enough with his rebellious daughter."

⊢||||

Joaquin's squad raced across Psyche's landscape, holding on for dear life and putting their fate into the hands of an AI.

"Joaquin, I have sent a signal to the chariots that should actuate the tracking display."

"Okay, Ada, I see it now. How did you do this? I cannot seem to get this suit to do anything. It seems to have a mind of its own."

"After you left the hangar, the chariots began to emit a comm signal matching a frequency programmed in my system by the UAE. It only became available when that hangar opened."

"Ada, I see the activity at the Achilles crater. What is that moving away from the crater and towards the base at hypervelocity?"

"Joaquin, my programming suggests that is undoubtedly an offensive weapon. Based on its trajectory, it will impact the base in three minutes."

"Three minutes, Ada? That's all? It just dawned on you to alert us of this *offensive* weapon now?"

Joaquin quickly cut Ada off and called his squads. "Charlie and Delta squad, continue to Achilles crater to assist Alpha and Bravo. Ada, set me on an intercept course with this projectile."

Credit: @Dedi5un

Sara and Salaam sat in the control room, watching the action unfold, searching frantically for any way to help. Sara, still frustrated that she could not reach out to her husband, begged Ada. "Ada, I'm only asking for a minute. Just connect me."

"Ms. Lafeete, I must inform you we have an incoming projectile intent on our mutual destruction arriving in three minutes. Commander McGeen's vital signs show he barely has three minutes left. We do not have time to connect."

"So, buddy, how does it feel to watch it all come crashing down around you? Any last words before your life's work melts into rock?"

"What happened to you, Lance? You were my best. You could have had a command. What does the old man have on you?"

"Have? Calager, you are the last person to care. Have? He has my respect. He would never hesitate to act against an adversary. He has courage. He has nothing on me."

"We were not at war. You knew that. The cat-and-mouse games we played in the depths of the oceans with those submarines were meant to prevent war. The game is to ping them to let them know we have been trailing them. You were going to destroy them. I did not give that order. The old man did not give that order. Lance, you were my XO, my best friend. We were navy men. Our job was to *prevent* war."

"Does that matter? They were not our allies. It would have looked like an accident. Order or not, the old man may not have vocalized his wishes, but he felt the same as I. It was time to end the game."

As Lance continued to banter on about justifying killing innocents, Calager was bleeding out. He barely had enough strength to move his legs and arms. But… maybe he had enough.

ꜩ꜡꜡꜡꜡

Joaquin struggled to pull his momentum weapon up to aim at the missile. Firing off three rounds to no avail, he called Ada. "Ada, I can't stop it. Our weapons are too weak. They will not even slow it down. Is there anything on board this flying chair that will? Otherwise, you and the rest of the base are toast."

"Joaquin, the only thing fast enough to catch up with that projectile with enough force to destroy it is your chariot."

ꜩ꜡꜡꜡꜡

Sara was at her wit's end. Damning Calager for his communication protocols during missions, she yelled at the AI, "Ada, if you do not put me through to Calager now, I'm pulling circuits."

"Sara, we have two squads in active combat with at least one squad down with no life signs and two more squads streaming across the asteroid to reach them. Protocol dictates no communication between non-combat personnel."

All Sara could do was slam her fists on the console and scream. "Adaaaaaa!"

Ada tracked everything in the combat zone at Achilles and the location of the projectile with urgency. She redirected all her programming from monitoring base functions to giving full attention to the emergency. At that nanosecond, she noticed something strange about Joaquin's chariot. It made no logical sense.

"Joaquin, I no longer have control of your chariot. What in the stars are you doing?"

"Ada, I finally figured out how to reason with this suit. It hurts like hell at first, but it works." Blood was still dripping down from Joaquin's temples where the suit interfaced with his mind. "You might want to warn anyone who decides to take a joy ride on a chariot that these suits have a mean frontal lobe jab. Some technomed neuro needle punched right into my skull and shot wires out beneath my forehead."

"Joaquin, stop!" Ada had increased her voice level tenfold to grab his attention. "You cannot do this. Your current course and speed have you colliding with the projectile in thirty seconds."

"Ada, that is the point."

"That's suicide, Joaquin." Ada fluctuated the frequency of her voice to simulate emotion.

Joaquin turned off the collision alert and mentally told his chariot of the Babylonian forge to accelerate. "No, Ada, that's sacrifice."

Calager had moved his arms and legs into position inch by inch as Lance had continued to banter on with ludicrous reasons justifying his actions. The blood from his gunshot wounds was pooling around his feet. Calager was questioning if he had properly prepared his people for this scenario. Covering every detail of a potential battle situation, begged for skills not every soldier could muster. *Did I train them to think for themselves? Can they evaluate the situation and create a solution? Heck, is anybody even alive out there?* Out of the corner of his eye, he thought he had found the answer.

Even if he had the time to act, he may not have the strength.

Salaam reached over to turn his monitor towards Sara as he gently touched her arm. "They have not stopped the projectile. The Achilles crater signals have gone dark. I think this is it."

"Salaam, it ain't over till it's over. Now, Ada, for the last time, punch me through to Calager!"

"Well, buddy, old pal, it's sayonara time." Lance raised his 9mm and placed the gun against Calager's helmet as his finger began to pull the trigger. Calager's blood loss began to slow his heartbeat, and his mind began to shut down. Not enough blood could course through his veins and arteries to keep him awake. Another bullet would not matter. He was dying.

Time crept almost to a halt as Joaquin approached the projectile. The chariot floated effortlessly within an arm's reach of the weapon of mass destruction. The chariot communicated to his mind that time was up. Joaquin turned to face the direction of the Achilles crater and saluted. "Adiós amigos. Suit, send this message to Sara. Weapon being diverted from direct impact. Cannot prevent communication blackout. See Shaahida's quarters for a flame and lens to guide the commander home."

Credit: @Dedi5un

A wave of destructive energy screamed across Psyche as the MAHEM device exploded. The electromagnetic pulse knocked out all communication, and the flash of light temporarily blinded everyone across the asteroid. The last wave of electrons from the base's communication system blasted into Calager's helmet. "Calager, I love…"

The voice of his one true love, his reason for living, struck deep into his soul. The adrenal glands on top of his kidneys began dumping massive amounts of cortisol and adrenaline into his bloodstream. The blood pressure in his body surged forward as his heart began to beat what little blood was left, charging oxygen and energy to activate his muscles. Neurons were firing across his mind as his senses flamed to life. Boulders were rising

to his left and right, racing towards his position. He could feel
their vibrations as they pounded the regolith. He could see his
adversary, the man who used to be his best friend, turn to see
what was coming as the trigger compressed and the firing pin
contacted the bullet.

Credit: @Dedi5un

The Excalibur lasers were firing across the crater as Shaahida
and the remaining members of the Alpha squad rushed Lance.
Two more of her squad dropped to the surface, drilled through
by lasers. Calager witnessed the transformation before his eyes as
the boulders became soldiers, and his mind told him Shaahida
was there. His body just reacted. There was no conscious
thought that he would remember, only instinct. Defend. Survive.

Calager lunged up off the crater's surface and slammed his palms against the barrel of the gun. The reaction force compressed the palms of his hands, activating the eight muscles in his forearms, then his biceps, and down into his obliques. The metal of the barrel collapsed on the end at the very moment the explosive gunpowder of the bullet reacted to the firing pin. With no exit at the end of the barrel, the force blew out in the opposite direction, shattering the breach face. Fragments flew out, shattering Lance's helmet, and bored deep into his brain.

Calager dropped to his knees suddenly as his thoughts returned to Sara. "McGeen to base, over? McGeen to base, over? Sara?"

Total silence.

Day three

Two troopers were left behind at the Achilles crater to secure the area and bury Lance's body. Shaahida, Calager, and the remaining members of Alpha were on their way back to base on their rovers, licking their wounds and mourning their losses. Their rovers had become hearses as they transported their dead back for a proper burial.

Shaahida looked down at Calager lying on the improvised rover bed with great respect. He would live not only because of his actions in battle but for his training of their units far in advance. When they arrived on Psyche, Calager had instituted a Valkyrie whole blood transfusion training program. He had made certain every squad was mixed with matching blood types, at least one member was O negative, and that they were trained on doing whole blood transfusions on the spot. Between the blood transfusions and the robot medic aboard, Calager had been patched up enough that he was somewhat stable for the moment.

"Still no response?" Calager whispered barely conscious. He had prepared himself for the worst after contact was lost with the base. There was a chance their lack of communication was the result of the electromagnetic pulse from the weapon. The alternative was unthinkable. The base could be gone.

"Not yet, sir. I'm sure it is a delay in getting communications back online." Shaahida was trying her best not to lose hope. Most of the Alpha squad and all of Bravo had been lost at Achilles. She had to hope their loss had some value. *We lost some fine soldiers in that crater.*

"I am sure you are right, Shaahida. That has got to be it." Shifting his weight off his bullet wound, he looked up to the stars towards what he figured was the rough direction of Earth.

Old man, you are willing to sacrifice your daughter? I will come for thee from the deep. Darkness will come for thee from the depths of my despair. Slow, frigid tentacles will ensnarl your heart and squeeze the very living water from your soul. At that last thought, Calager lost his battle to sleep.

𒌋𒌋𒌋

"Sir, wake up, sir. We are back." Back to what, Shaahida was not certain, but as they crested the crater's rim to view the base below, her thoughts were answered.

Darkness, like the depths of a black hole, blanketed the area. The base crater's metallic mineral sparkle had been forever shadowed. The MAHEM device had melted the surrounding landscape into the dark black of hell. All surface structures were gone. Their laser communication array, growth zones, and exterior fuel reservoirs had been melted into metallic rock.

"It is all just black. There are no distinguishing characteristics of the base visible. Sir, I cannot even find the front door."

Calager stood in the rover, shaking off his slumber as anger flushed through his veins. Every fiber of his being shook with rage as he screamed, "Sara!" He slumped to the floor, sobbing, "I have failed you."

The remaining squad members of the UAE Psyche mission all turned away from the direction of the base, lost in their thoughts. They were afraid of what else they might see. Family.

Friends. Home. Gone. Shaahida knew the commander had very little energy left before he lost consciousness again. It would be up to her to give the last few soldiers hope and lead them. *Lead? Ha. My first full command will be to lead a few lost souls to an escape ship on the far side of this dark rock. We barely have enough of the right blood type between us to get the commander back on his feet. Hope?*

"All right, troopers, let's move this rover around to these coordinates..." Before she could finish, something flashed in the corner of her eye. She looked around the rover but could not determine the cause. *PTSD? Great, how am I going to lead if I lose it now?* Shaahida knew the battle at Achilles was not long past. The laser flashes burning holes through her squad were still very fresh in her mind. Trying to snap herself out of it, she continued, "Drive to these coordinates and prepare to disembark..." Another flash.

Through the storms, I call to thee. Through the darkness, I shine for thee. Be not afraid. Come home to me, ye in the dark. Follow my light. The words came to Shaahida like a cool ocean breeze gracing the shore after a hot summer's day. She knew that light. It was the harbinger of hope during a storm. *A lighthouse?* Turning back to what used to be the base, she waited. There it came again. Hope. As the light flashed out from the darkness, for an instant, she could feel what connected Sara and Calager. Love like no other beamed outwards from the base, flashing across the dark of night, a lighthouse calling them home. Somewhere deep within that melted landscape of rock and metal, they had survived.

She realized, still trying to shake off the trauma from the battle, she had let her emotions get the best of her. *Of course,* she thought. *Joaquin's impact with the weapon must have diverted it from a direct impact with the base. We may have lost all surface structures from the energy wave, but the sublevels of the base must still be intact.*

Memorial – one year later

It was a somber gathering that day as the sun slowly approached the horizon. Calager searched the vast hall, finding Sara and Salaam quietly discussing something in a corner. What was left of his military detachment gathered in full ceremonial uniform. They stood at rest in orderly rows and columns at the front of the newly erected greenhouse dome. This was thanks in part to supplies sent by the UAE, which included a 3D construction printer. All heads bowed as one. Replacements would be arriving soon for their lost members. The sun's rays bounced off the shining metal and glass, raining prism rainbows down upon the capsule. Emblazed into the capsule was the name Joaquin Gonzalez, with an image of a Chariot of the Babylonian Forge in the background. Behind the capsule were hundreds of rows of new seedlings stretching to reach the light.

Credit: @Dedi5un

Calager approached the capsule, resting his palm there a moment and then turned to face the gathering. "A harbinger of hope in the darkness after a terrible storm. That was Joaquin's last wish. As he approached the MAHEM device, he knew of its destructive powers. His last message to us was one of respect and one of hope. He saluted his friends, showing his respect. He reminded us of a method of communication that could survive the onslaught of an electromagnetic pulse – a simple candle flame used to alert ships for thousands of years.

"Chile's first astronaut and I imagine one of many heroes to come, Joaquin gave us a flame that will never be extinguished. Though I still have some investigations as to where this open flame candle originated…" Calager glanced towards Shaahida and Sara with an ever so slight smile on his lips. "This everlasting flame of life that was so ingeniously put to use as a focused beacon of light, alerting us that our home still existed, will never be extinguished."

Commander Calager McGeen stepped back in precise military fashion and snapped his polished shoes together, bringing his body to full military attention. The creased lines of his uniform flowed straight as arrows. He performed a left face, facing those of his command and bellowed out, "Squad! Attention! Right face!" The remaining troops assigned to Psyche snapped to attention, spun on the heels of their left feet, and snapped their feet together again, facing the capsule. "Present! Arms!" Before the thunderous echoes of their feet had left the hall, their arms swept through the air, snapping to attention in a salute to their fallen comrade.

Shaahida marched forward and placed a small lit candle down into an open compartment on the capsule. She pushed a small button on the control panel and snapped to attention again, saluting the capsule. The capsule moved forward and down through a tube beneath the hall. Everyone held their breath. The only sound was the quiet hiss of the air circulation system. Then, a very quiet click emanated from beneath the hall. At once, the entire hall was ablaze in light.

Calager faced the crowd again. "Ladies and gentlemen. Let me present the first fully operational growth zone on the UAE's Joaquin Gonzalez forward base of stellar operations."

Shaahida stood at the head of the table, tapping the spoon against the glass to command everyone's attention. She nodded toward Calager, but he quickly spoke, "No, Shaahida, this honor is yours."

"He sacrificed his life for his friends, his family. Diverting the MAHEM device at the last moment gave us all a chance. It was a sacrifice that I, for one, will never take for granted. This feast is in his honor. This will be the first of many harvests over the years. A toast to Joaquin!" They all raised their glasses to Joaquin. Spread across the breakfast table were piles of blueberry pancakes, muffins, and packets of blueberry juice.

Calager leaned over to Shaahida as he glanced across the table. "Joaquin would have appreciated this, Shaahida. This is a job well done. You still owe me. I expect to see you on the mat at oh five hundred again tomorrow. A regulation is a regulation. Open flames are never permitted in our quarters."

Sara, stuffing her mouth with pancakes covered in blueberry syrup, elbowed him to relent. Some commotion at the end of the table gathered all their attention. Salaam looked in their direction in dismay as his appetite had gotten the best of him. His overzealous pile of pancakes and muffins had toppled to the table. As they noticed his predicament, they all just erupted into laughter.

Calager kept his thoughts of the destruction of millions of lives on the Earth to himself. Only a few knew of the chain reactions rippling through the freshwater supplies of the Earth triggered by a single random neutrino. A trillion-to-one chance had become a reality as an abomination created by humans turned against them. He knew today was a time to celebrate a lost friend, but he struggled with the reality before him. He was faced with an impossible mission; jumpstart some ancient ship and transport millions from Earth to another star system to save humanity.

I know the name and the face of our enemy. We are the enemy. Are we worth saving?

The End.

Acknowledgments:

Behind every good author, there is an editor. The words would not have made sense without my editor, Silja Evelyn. Thank you for your patience and your guidance. To @Dedi5un, the chief illustrator and cover artist for this collection, your talents are amazing. Thank you for taking the time to read and imagine art to carry the words forward. A young lady, Ryan Boatman, also deserves a hat tip for her great artist impressions.

Also from the author:

GENSHIP trilogy

Book One - NUERA1

Book Two - The Last Holy See

Book Three - Joshua's Law

What is next for Henry Sipes?

We will return to asteroid 16 Psyche with the novel, Thatenbia, coming in early 2025.

Visit www.henry-sipes.com for more information.